SAVING *BEN TRE*

By D. R. Van Wye

Tina & Patrick,

Peace blessings
for you and the
children. I hope lessons
count in the future.

Uncle Dave

SAVING BEN TRE

Published by D. R. Van Wye
ISBN: 1500384992
ISBN 13: 978-1500384999
Library of Congress Control Number: 2014911960
CreateSpace Independent Publishing Platform
North Charleston, South Carolina
Published in the USA
Permission: The "Memorial Day Prayer" is reprinted with the kind permission of Reverend Barbara Pescan.

The characters in this story are fictitious and are not intended to represent actual people.

For my family
and
Those who have served
and
Those who do serve

"Youth is easily deceived because it is quick to hope."
—Aristotle

———

"When those who must do the fighting have
the right to decide between war and peace,
history will no longer be written in blood."
—Immanuel Kant

ACKNOWLEDGMENTS

My thanks to family and friends for reading all or part of the manuscript and providing advice and encouragement. I am grateful to Elizabeth, Gretchen, Brian, Marcia and Alice Van Wye for reading early drafts and making helpful suggestions. For thoughtful encouragement and counsel I thank Jean Martin and Neill Cowles. I especially thank my wife, Elizabeth, an accomplished writer, for her insightful and constructive review and advice.

I also want to recognize several authors who have written influential, informative, and inspiring works. Siegfried Sassoon, in *Memoirs of an Infantry Officer,* describes the moral courage of a combat infantry officer who protests the prolonged suffering of World War I. Stanley Karnow wrote *Vietnam, A History, The First Complete Account of Vietnam at War,* a comprehensive and enlightening history of America's war in Vietnam, with remarkable clarity and detail on how the decisions and actions of leaders in America and Vietnam resulted in conflict. Retired Army Lieutenant General Phillip B.

Davidson's book, *Vietnam at War*, describes the war with a well-developed military insight and shows how the United States lost the war to the "superior strategy" of the North Vietnamese. The book, *Patriots: The Vietnam War Remembered From All Sides*, written by Christian G. Appy, gives a balanced presentation of compelling perspectives on the war from over one hundred people who lived through it.

TABLE OF CONTENTS

MEKONG DELTA
VIETNAM
(For illustration only)

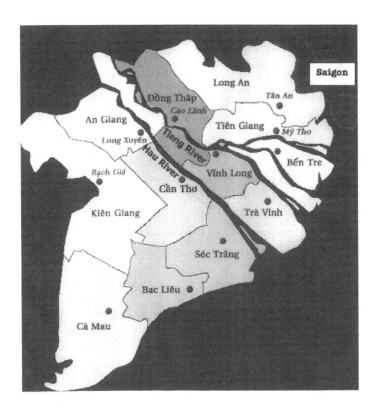

CAPTAIN BLAKE'S SKETCH

Shows Ben Tre within range of Viet Cong rockets from the Huu Dinh Forest area, the approach of the lien doi (infantry) battalion from the west, and the three abandoned forts they occupy as they clear and interdict the VC in the area north of Ben Tre.

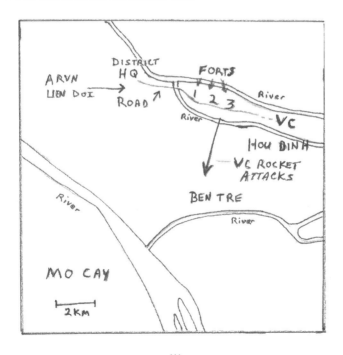

One

OCTOBER 1970: DECISION

"The best time for the Viet Cong to hit us is when this plane lands," declares Jack Aims matter-of-factly while looking out the small fuselage window. He's the stout, thick-armed man in the seat next to me. Turning his head to me he adds, "They don't call it rocket alley for nuthin'." The Boeing 707 jet is full of GIs headed for a landing at Bien Hoa Airbase, South Vietnam. It has been a long flight from the big army processing center at Oakland California to this notorious war in Vietnam.

"Nice of you to mention that, Jack," I say while trying to see what's out the window. He's another lieutenant I know from training at Fort Benning, Georgia. The plane banks slightly and I have a bird's eye view of the big base, laid out over many acres of the flat land northeast of Saigon. I can clearly see a reassuringly, heavily fortified defensive perimeter made of concrete bunkers, sandbagged trenches, and barbed wire supported by M113 armored personnel carriers. Those are the ones with the big old .50-caliber heavy machine gun mounted on top. I know the place gets hit with 122-millimeter rockets or mortars every couple of weeks, but I figure the odds are not too bad for our landing. This confining, hurtling tube needs to land fast, I think. We need to get out of this high-priced coffin and near some protective dirt, the refuge of infantrymen.

I'm Donald Van Howe, a green ROTC second lieutenant squeezed into this Boeing 707 with a whole bunch of other butter bar lieutenants like me and about a hundred and fifty young GIs even greener than I am. If anyone were to look at me sitting next to dark haired, stocky Jack Aims they would see that the army takes all types. I am six feet tall, with brown hair cut short with a part, blue eyes, and a lean frame. I am trying to keep a little weight around the middle as a reserve in case I am captured and food is scarce, plus I don't like to miss a meal. Actually, the airplane is full of guys of all different types and sizes-tall, short, heavy, thin, with afros, crew cuts, a full cross section of young men. Some of us are in green Class-A uniforms and some are in khakis. While picturing Viet Cong rockets hitting the runway, the back of my mind registers that my green wool uniform, comfortable in this air-conditioned cabin, will be sweating hot when we get out on the tarmac. I wish I were in battle fatigues right now.

Sensing the plane tilt forward for its final approach I wonder how soon it will turn around and head back to the United States. When this jet goes back to the world, it will be called a freedom bird by every lucky soul aboard, ecstatic with the knowledge that they had endured the cauldron of forces that threatened their every living moment—rifle and machine gun bullets, booby traps, full-scale assaults by the enemy, and exploding rockets, mortars, or grenades. Or worse, capture followed by confinement in a tiger cage, torture, starvation, and a lonely death in an unknown location far away from family and friends, obliterated from any meaningful existence and lost to the world. For our destination, this plane is not a freedom bird.

The voice on the intercom says for the second time, "Make sure you fasten your seatbelts."

I laugh to myself wondering if a plane crash would be worse than where any of us might be going. Everyone on board knows it could be a one-way trip. How many here will go back home in a body bag? My mind plays the tune from Country Joe and the Fish about parents seeing their boy come home in a box. Even facing that, most of the guys think there are worse things. Like being messed up so bad that you are unable to lead a normal life, or being proven a coward. Everyone on the plane can say they stood up to be counted when Uncle Sam called, whether they wanted to or not. They may have considered running to Canada, taking advantage of family connections, or hiding behind some legal excuse. Whether they volunteered or their draft number came up, they stood up, showed up, signed up, and now they are here.

The plane touches down, tires bumping on the runway, engines roaring in reverse to slow our rush forward. No VC rockets hit the airfield—a lucky day. We have arrived in South Vietnam to meet our destiny. When the cabin door opens, the heat and humidity welcome us like the moist breath of a giant reptile hovering over the asphalt.

I turn to Jack, and say, "Here we are in a tropical paradise, guests of President Thieu and the Army of the Republic of Vietnam, the ARVN."

Jack smiles and quips, "Ha, this heat is the Nam sucking you into hell."

"Yeah, Jack, being from Virginia you know about heat."

"True," he says, "Lynchburg can warm up a bit."

A crack comes from back in the line. "Hey, this is first class, a free ride to a foreign country, a regular tourist destination."

"At least we had a safe landing," I say, as we step down a long flight of stairs and walk across the tarmac to waiting buses.

We get to a long bunkhouse, a military barracks, Vietnam style—wood sided halfway up, screens to the roof of tin sheets. Sandbags are laid up against the walls. Sandbags also cover the rooftop in case of rocket attack. A pleasant surprise awaits inside—standard issue, steel-frame bunk beds with genuine army striped mattresses, thin but a lot better than sleeping on the ground, a real luxury compared to the muddy, sandbagged fighting positions we saw on the perimeter of this huge base. There is even a convenient sandbag bunker for cover in an enemy attack.

Back in the barracks, after picking up our standard issue of jungle fatigues, boots, socks, and boxer shorts, all in olive drab, Jack and I get out of our heavy green uniforms and gladly put on the cooler jungle garb.

Jack says, "Hey, Van, with these new duds I feel like we're gonna be here for a while."

"Yeah, very inviting," I answer.

He pins an olive-colored, metal lieutenant's bar on his boonie hat and says, "Nice to get subdued insignia to pin on—don't want to be a target."

I watch him pin on his rank and the black metal crossed rifles of the infantry officers and reflect on the men in years before us who were easy targets because they wore colorful yellow stripes, gold and silver bars, and other glittering devices. "Makes you feel all dressed up and ready to go, don't it?" I say.

Jack tips his head back and laughs. "Ha! Let's find out what's going on."

In our new uniforms, we walk over to an open area between buildings where we are to gather for an orientation. A big man with sunglasses, short afro haircut, baseball cap, and fatigues with subdued second-lieutenant bars stands there looking like he knows what is going on. Other guys mill around doing the usual smoking and joking while waiting for the orientation.

Jack and I walk up to the big man who gives us a knowing look. "You guys look like you just got here."

"Yeah," Jack says, "how about you?"

"Got here yesterday."

As we shake hands, he says, "My name is Shepard, but most people call me Shep."

We exchange names, hometowns, and other small talk about stateside assignments.

With a sweeping hand gesture Shep says, "On this big base with a heavily defended perimeter there should be no serious problems with Victor Charles, other than rockets or a few mortar shells."

When he mentions Victor Charles, I know it is GI slang for Viet Cong, the term widely used for guerilla fighters opposing our allies in South Vietnam. The phonetic alphabet used by the military in radio talk uses the terms Victor and Charlie to clearly say the letters V and C. Soldiers inevitably turn this into several variations of Nam lingo like Charles, Charlie, Mr. Charles, and Chuck.

Shep gives us the lowdown. He says we are going to have a choice of assignment between a US unit and a field team working with a Vietnamese unit. That means you can either work with US troops or on a Mobile Advisory Team (MAT) with the Field Advisory Element, Military Assistance Command, Vietnam (MACV). Just then, a captain shows up and calls for attention. He instructs us to file into a building with benches for an orientation.

The briefing confirms what Shep said about the choice of assignments. A lot of things are running through my mind. This is a choice with big differences. On a MAT, you are in a five-man team that lives and works with a Vietnamese field unit, usually a platoon or company. In an American unit I would be a platoon leader with twenty to forty men assigned to a company of several platoons. This, in turn, would be part of a battalion of several companies, which is part of larger and larger military units up to a division or more. On the one hand, the American system provides higher echelons of support with all of the attendant resources and firepower. On the other hand a MAT team is part of a military hierarchy that parallels the political-military system of the Republic of Vietnam. Organized into a system of provinces, districts, villages, and hamlets under the control of corresponding chiefs, many Vietnamese counterparts of advisors are political leaders rather than proven soldiers promoted through the ranks.

Everyone in the briefing is looking forward, paying attention, trying to pick up every detail of units where they could be assigned and searching for every nuance of the latest army pitch on the state of the war. Each knows that in a matter of hours their fate will be sealed by marching orders. No one here will be sitting on a bench in a secure room. Who will get lucky with a dream assignment? Who will be engulfed in a living hell like the worst nightmare?

The back of my mind churns over the possibilities. I can picture advisors out in the jungle with a platoon of local Vietnamese soldiers. What are they saying to each other? Can we trust them? Are they related to VC? Will they stand and fight? I see us under attack by VC. As soon as the enemy firing intensifies, our guys turn around and run like crazy back through the jungle leaving two or three advisors there, firing M16s like mad, being surrounded by Viet Cong, and killed or taken prisoner, trapped, starved, and tortured in a tiger cage.

If working with the Vietnamese is chancy, there are big problems too with many American units. Unwilling recruits wind up in Nam because of their low draft lottery numbers. Some accept their fate, and others are bitter and resentful of their bad luck. With troop withdrawals and peace negotiations in Paris, no one wants to be the last man to die in a war that many see as useless. It's hard to blame 'em for a bad attitude. And, there are problems with drugs, racial issues, and rumors of officers who will sacrifice men to get their career tickets punched. I don't know how widespread all this is, but I do know its bad for morale and discipline and the incidents of insubordination, mutiny, and refusing orders are on the rise.

In the briefing room people shift on the hard, creaking benches. Realizing that his audience is getting restless, the briefing officer winds up the part about advisory efforts and continues with a slide listing American units. I imagine being out in the boondocks with twenty or thirty American soldiers who are unhappy with their mission to patrol an area several kilometers away from their base. Most of them are good guys, but there are a few hardheads who are disgruntled beyond reasoning. Out in the jungle, I am just trying to do the job and get them back in one piece. I know we are going to be out on night perimeter defense, taking turns keeping watch, and trying to get some sleep. I've heard about fragging— the death of an unwanted officer or NCO by "accident" or "enemy action" when actually killed by their own troops. A grenade exploding or a "stray" rifle shot is blamed on an enemy attack.

Thinking about this gives me the creeps. It isn't just army statistics on low morale and discipline. It's also personal. I knew an officer it happened to. He and I had served in the same battalion back at Fort Carson. Bill Star was a West Point graduate, sharp, and regarded as a man who had a bright future. He left for Nam one month before I did. Making flight connections in the Charleston airport on my way to jungle school, I learned the news about Bill Star. He had been on patrol with his platoon and was shot in the back. He is dead. His shocking loss is real.

———

Later, I am on the chow line with Shep and Jack, waiting to get into the mess hall.

"So, gents," I say, "what are you gonna sign up for?"

"MAT," Shep says, "because I like the idea of a different culture and I hear there are many good Vietnamese units. It's their country, so they should be fighting for it more than us."

Jack chimes in. "There is no way I'm going to a US unit. Not with all the problems I hear about. What about you, Van?"

"I'd rather take my chances on a MAT team. Five reliable men are better than dealing with all of the problems in a regular American unit. Five guys on a MAT team have a clear-cut area of responsibility and, being stuck out in the boonies, we'll stick together and survive."

Shep says, "You know, a lot of the guys here are saying that going to a MAT team is crazy risky. They think there is safety in a big American unit."

"The herd instinct is powerful," Jack notes, "but it is better to die with a weapon in your hands fighting an overwhelming enemy than being shot in the back."

I nod my head. "You are not safe anywhere in this country. I think I'll take my chances with a MAT team."

———

That evening, some of us newbies are sitting around the barracks going over our jungle gear, writing letters home, and generally enjoying a moment of peace. We will soon be scattered about the Republic of Vietnam as replacements for those who are going home in a big freedom bird, or those unfortunates headed to the burial detachment at Dover Air Force Base, or maybe those who are now prisoners of the Hanoi regime.

Two other lieutenants, Snyder and Lanahan, have bunks near me, Jack, and Shep. Snyder has dark brown, curly hair and an athletic, medium build. Lanahan's hair is a short-cropped, thick, sandy blond. He has the tall, thin frame of a distance runner. I remember them from Fort Benning because they took a deal from the army—if you volunteer for two tours in Vietnam, you go to Airborne and Ranger Schools and make captain in two years. Airborne rangers are qualified to parachute from aircraft, and they are also graduates of a tough, elite infantry course.

Snyder and Lanahan are standing in the isle between rows of bunks, smoking Camels near a red butt can hanging on a four by four support post. Sitting on the edge of his bunk, polishing his boots, Jack looks over and asks, "What did you guys sign up for?"

Lanahan blows smoke out of his nostrils. Pointing to Snyder with his chin, he replies, "We both requested the 101st Airborne Division."

Snyder nods in agreement and says, "Hey, Jack, I heard you are going to be an advisor to the Vietnamese. That true?"

"Yeah, me, Shep, Van, and a few others," answers Jack.

Sitting on our bunks, Shep and I look up to see how Snyder and Lanahan will respond.

Lanahan flicks his cigarette ashes into the red can and says, "I think Rangers do risky stuff, but you guys will be way out there in the boonies with no US troops. Do you think ARVN is going to protect you?"

"Well," says Shep, "maybe if we're advisin' them right it will be OK."

My letter writing interrupted, I chime in, "Yeah, it's Nixon's Vietnamization plan where they take on a bigger role. As long as they're not VC sympathizers or turntails we'll be fine."

"Yeah," says Lanahan, "that's what I'm worried about. I'd rather be with our own guys with beaucoup echelons of support."

Snyder pipes up. "I have to say, I do worry about the dedication of our own troops. You know, with the drugs and discipline problems. I just hope things will be strac in an Airborne unit."

Taking in this conversation, I realize we all know that strac means that a unit is strong, tough, and ready for combat. I agree that Airborne units are probably like that.

"Ain't much strac in the Nam right now," says Shep sitting on the edge of his bunk, head shaking, and eyes looking down at the concrete floor.

"Sure," says Lanahan, "we may have a few pot smokers and dopers, but the men will be well trained and there won't be any conscientious objectors."

"What do you mean?" replies Jack, a surprised tone in his voice.

Lanahan tosses his cigarette butt in the red can and looks directly at Jack. "I mean guys that are too chicken to fight, like antiwar hippies and draft resisters."

I say, "It sounds like you've been hearin' stories, you know, about guys that won't do the job when you need 'em."

"Yeah, and I won't put up with it," Lanahan says.

"General Patton would get his butt fragged in the Nam," says Shep. "Better check it out before trying to do what the higher ups can't do."

Jack says, "You actually might be lucky to have a conscientious objector in your platoon. Some of those guys are braver and tougher than a whole squad armed to the teeth. Did you know there are COs who got the Medal of Honor?

"Naah, how could that be?" asks Lanahan.

"Some COs serve without carrying a gun, like medics and support roles," answers Jack. "They are out there with the frontline troops saving their butts under hostile fire. They can get it worse than most grunts. Ever hear about Desmond Doss in the 77th Infantry Division during World War II?"

Lanahan shakes his head sideways and mutters, "Nah."

After pausing, Jack continues, "He risked his life to rescue wounded men under fire. Way beyond the call of duty. There is even a highway named after him around Lynchburg where I grew up."

At first, Lanahan looks at Jack with mouth agape, and then he turns tight-lipped. He says to Jack, "I didn't know."

Jack says, "Yeah, not many do. Since he is a local hero in Lynchburg, I heard about him a lot. Heard about others like him too. There was a CO, he served here in Nam near Plieku. I think his name was Bennett. Nixon awarded him a posthumous CMH a few months ago for risking his life pulling wounded to safety. People like that, any unit would be lucky to have 'em."

"We hear so much against the war I just felt if someone is not for me then he's against me. I guess it's not that simple," says Lanahan.

"You gotta know where someone is coming from," says Shep. "A CO has to believe it's wrong to kill in all wars...not just this war."

"Yeah," says Jack "Its about the morality of war. Think about it. Take away conscience and you destroy society. I've got a lot of respect for those guys."

After listening intently to this exchange I speak up. "I never heard about medics who won the Congressional Medal of Honor, but I have heard about other deserving COs."

I pause and they all look at me.

"I know a conscientious objector who's not in the military. He's doing work in a hospital as an alternative to military service. He has strong beliefs and will live or die by them. I can respect that kind of integrity."

Jack nods, "I think courage comes in many forms. Real courage means standing up for what you believe no matter what."

"Amen," says Shep.

Lanahan just looks at us with a thoughtful expression on his face.

After a quiet time of folding socks, packing duffle bags, smoking, and joking, we hit the rack. Tomorrow, we all head out to our assignments.

Two

FIRST NIGHT

Tonight, sleep is not easy. Anxiety smolders inside of me. I guess I am unsettled by the whirl of new experiences and a feeling of impending doom about being here in this so called quagmire of South Vietnam, poised to plunge into the gloomy vortex that will change my life forever.

I still feel the wrenching loss of saying goodbye to my wife Cathy and baby daughter back in the States. I had lifted my daughter up in the air and saw her innocent face against the bright blue sky. I closed my eyes and hoped that she would have a healthy and good life and that I would return to see her grow up. With her back in my wife's arms, we all hugged for one last time. The separation and loss tears at my gut and weakens my resolve to be here.

Lying in the darkened bunkroom I vaguely think that any moment a rush of incoming rockets and mortars

17

will come crashing onto the roof and all around the compound. I recall that it may not be safe to run for the bunkers. Mamasans who work here can be agents of the enemy known to set booby traps that have killed GI's diving for cover. What a place! But it is not the chance of rocket attack that bothers me so much as the haunting thoughts about my own mettle. Will I be tough enough, brave enough, or have enough resolve to make it? I can really admire the daring and tenacity of the three hundred Spartans led by Leonidas at Thermopylae.

A little moonlight filters in through the screens. I can see orderly lines of sleeping forms on the top and bottom bunks, set in long rows on both sides of the room. A guy several bunks down opposite me flips onto his side and slides off the top bunk carefully, not disturbing the sleeping man on the bottom. He heads down the aisle for the door at the end of the building, no doubt for a smoke or a call of nature. I hope there are no trip wires and grenades set to blow when he opens the latrine door. What if rockets come in at an awkward moment?

Restlessly, I flip over and try to bury my head in the pillow. I hear Frankie Valli and the Four Season's song in my in my mind, "Walk Like a Man," even though it is about a woman and not about war. The lyrics of Bob Dylan pop into my mind too. I don't know how many roads a man walks down before he's a man. But, yes, I want to walk like a man.

I remember an uncle who was in World War I, and my dad served in the Pacific as a navy officer in World War II. A forbearer even served in the American Revolution. Would I be as good as all of the soldiers who had gone before me, in Vietnam or in any other war?

Why can't this war be like those? In other wars there were more clear-cut reasons to fight and more of a national effort. Does this Vietnam thing make sense?

President Kennedy's words about serving your country are an inspiration to me. In spite of all my worries, pros and cons, serving seems right. But, I hope it is for a higher purpose, for something good. Now I just walk like a blind man who does not know the truth with the tangle of conflicts and confusion. I just have to screw my courage to the sticking point and deal with what's in front of me.

I turn over again on the bunk. The screen door opens and the guy who answered the call of nature walks in. There were no explosions. He survived a trip to the latrine, a successful mission in the Nam. The moon is up, brightening this imperfect sanctuary. It shines on us. It also shines on the Viet Cong. It is a peaceful moment. My mind is still on alert, standing guard duty through the night. Can I go through a 365-day tour like this? If I can't get some sleep I won't survive.

A hopeful thought comes to me. I have to be confident in my army training. Surely that is enough to see me through. Maybe I have learned a few things in four years of ROTC and almost a year of stateside duty at Fort Carson with the Fifth Mechanized Infantry. But I know that my most significant military achievement is graduation from the jungle school at Fort Sherman in Panama as a Jungle Expert. A couple of weeks of misery doing combat maneuvers on a jungle floor covered with several inches of mud, puncturing our hands on black thorn trees, poking right through a leather glove, and coping with the rainy season, taught me more than all the rest.

The jungle school instructors ran us over one hill after the other, through mock Vietnamese villages, over walls, down ropes, across steams, and through thick vegetation, all while avoiding nasty serpents. They showed us the survival arts of eating snakes, rappelling down cliffs, and dealing with snipers and VC sympathizers. They ran us through obstacles for days and days, keeping us from sleep and rest and adding to our fatigue. "If you don't learn this you will die in Vietnam" was the constant refrain.

My mind flashes back to a perimeter guard watch out in the jungle in pouring rain. We rotated a two-hour guard shift between three bone-tired and miserable men. Captured students would be subjected to prisoner of war conditions so it was important for the guard to stay awake. I peered at the luminescent dial of my watch through the dark, wet night and saw the hands creep around too slowly during each interminable, uncomfortable moment. It was luxury to be relieved at guard and then to sink back into six inches of mud with rain pouring down all over me to catch some much coveted sleep.

The next day I was on a team that victoriously met the challenge of swimming the Rio Chagres. We were divided into four-man teams with at least one non-swimmer in each. The task was to swim our equipment across the river, maybe a distance of two hundred feet, where sharks had been spotted on occasion. We made a poncho raft with brush inside to float the rifles, packs, boots, and other gear and to provide buoyancy for our nonswimmer. This all had to be towed across the river with a swift six-mile-per-hour current. It was not enough to just get across the river. To claim success we had to reach a specific point on the opposite bank.

We stood by the rushing waters looking at the muddy bank on the other side. But, tired from our multiple days of humping through the jungle, we were excited by the challenge of making it across the river and figured our splashing would scare the sharks away. A dip in the water held another attraction. We were covered with mud from sleeping on the jungle floor so it was a chance to clean off. We decided to go for it.

As the lead swimmer, I took hold of one corner of our raft and aimed for a point far above our intended landing to compensate for the current. We pushed out into the swiftly moving water and were soon stroking vigorously. Halfway across we were being pushed quickly downstream. Shouting encouragement to each other we stroked harder with arms and legs thrashing through the water. We could see a root growing out right at our designated mark but it looked like we would miss it. Realizing how close it would be, we swam for all we were worth. Just as we were passing the mark, I lunged for the root stretching my arms to grab it with a few fingers. Water washed over my head, while I kept a grip on the raft. For a moment I feared that we would be swept free but the furious kicking of our team held us there, and we thrashed the raft into the shore. An instructor Captain walked over to us, his boots standing on the bank above our heads. He looked at us lying in exhaustion on the muddy bank, worn out, wet, river rats, and he said, "You made it, that's twenty-five points."

Later that day we learned that two of our classmates had broken legs or backs while training on a high rope slide over the river from a cliff to the opposite bank. We all had to do the same slide, about two hundred feet long, so this news got our attention. When these two classmates got to the other side, they did not stop in time to avoid hitting a tree. Some of the guys said the two injured lieutenants were lucky because now they did not have to go to the Nam.

As jungle school drew to a close we knew that we would soon be in Nam. Talk and attitudes became grimmer. It wasn't just the news of all the fighting, casualties, death, and destruction; it was also the bizarre nature of the war itself. The longer we were at school, the more we learned about the threats we would face: villagers who sympathized with the VC would turn against you, and there were booby traps, land mines, pungi pits, sappers, snipers, rockets, mortars, hot landing zones, and other deadly things. We were going into a maelstrom and there was no place to hide. It put a cold knot in your gut.

With sleep still eluding me, I realize that my focus and attention in jungle school had been better than almost any other time in my life. The instructors, veterans of the war themselves, got my attention because I believed what they said. My diploma with green snakes on it signified I had passed the test. Too bad the patch was not in stock at the commissary. I think the patch would look good on my uniform and show that I had some useful military experience compared to the reality of my inexperience.

After sorting out these thoughts I am a little more relaxed now. Someone down the row of bunks coughs quietly. A little cool night air drifts in through the screen windows easing the discomfort of the almost incessant heat. I think of the young soldier I met on the airplane coming here and wonder how he is doing on his first night in Vietnam.

I had risen from my seat and was walking in the aisle toward the back of the airplane. It felt good to stretch my legs. A young soldier was sitting about halfway back to the tail of the plane. He, too, was wearing the green uniform, and not the khaki worn by most. We were all young soldiers, but the difference of a few years between nineteen and twenty-four seemed large. At twenty-four, after college, after a year in the army I felt like a man of the world.

As I approached he looked up and I said, "Hello, soldier."

"Hello, sir," he responded as all privates are taught to respond to an officer.

Looking at the tight contours of his narrow face, and his brown, weepy eyes, I said, "How ya doin'?"

"I'm worried about the Nam, sir. I hear it's bad and I don't want to die there."

"Yeah," I said in a truly sympathetic tone reflecting my commiseration.

Pausing, with the sound of the jet engines filling the moment, a whole series of thoughts jumped into my mind. I thought, at age eighteen or nineteen he is still close to the fold of his parent's home and the support of his hometown friends. His army experience has been wrenching; he has been torn between a loving upbringing and being thrust into a war beyond his control.

I said, "We'll see what it's like when we get there. Maybe you'll get a good assignment."

He squinted at my name tag. "Lieutenant Van Howe, if I could cut off my arm right now so I won't have to go, I would do it," he said, his eyes downcast.

"I know what you mean," I answered, knowing his admission of fear was an honest, straightforward, man-to-man expression of a true feeling that got my respect.

I could feel an echo of his fear in my own gut. Everyone on the airplane had that fear. Somehow we deal with it, with our own ability to cope.

Trying to let him know that his fears are normal, I said, "I know guys who broke bones in jungle school and were glad to get out of going to Nam. A lot of guys think they are lucky."

"Yeah, that's it." He nods. "That's the way to get out alive."

I recalled Henry Fleming with his "Red Badge of Courage," and wondered if this young soldier would feel braver, like Henry, if he had a wound to show off, a wound that said he sacrificed for his country, a wound that other men envied, that made him stand out as a soldier who had been close to death and who was esteemed in the eyes of others. There is a fine balance here between life and death, courage and cowardice, shame and self- esteem. The "red badge" could build up a crumpled courage, or it could provide an honorable excuse for a ticket out of the bloody madness of war.

Not knowing what else to say, I asked him where he was from, where he went to basic training, how he liked the army. He said he was from New Jersey, dropped out of college and got drafted, went to basic at Fort Benning.

He said the army takes you away from better things in life, but service is the right thing if your country gives you a specific invitation like a draft notice. It's just fate.

Seeing that he was feeling a little better I said, "I've got to hit the head. Just take it one step at a time. Good luck to you."

"Good luck to you too, lieutenant. Thanks for stopping by."

It's a nice memory. Maybe I helped the guy feel better. Finally, my mind is slowing down. Tossing and turning in the squeaky bunk, I feel I am not in a dream. This is really happening. But, I have not lost the connection to the home and family I have left behind. I feel more confident. There are a few hours left until dawn. Drifting off to sleep I am ready for what comes tomorrow.

Three

TRUONG SON PATRIOTS

Dang Vu Hiep walks swiftly but carefully on the trail from his home in Trung Lap Hamlet. He is dressed like the few farmers who are also traveling on the trail, loose-fitting, black garments, conical straw hat, and sandals cut from rubber tires. The hat shades his high cheekbones, wide nose and the flat but slightly upturned lips of his mouth. It covers his coarse black hair. He is half-a-head taller than most Vietnamese and self-consciously worries that he will be noticed. He carries a straw basket so it appears that he has been to the market. His secret is that he is on his way to the nearby tunnels of Cu Chi. Excitement and joy fill him as he anticipates meeting new comrades from the North who will team up with him on a special mission in the Mekong Delta. This new mission is his reward for repeated successes in leading raids against the Americans and their South Vietnamese allies. He almost bounds enthusiastically down the trail, yet a voice in his head tells him to watch out for American soldiers and helicopters known to be in the area.

Upon arriving at a familiar location he slows down and listens. The wind rustles, gently shifting tree branches. The ominous, soft *whup, whup* of a distant helicopter flows over the treetops. Ducking into a thicket of vegetation Hiep finds a hole covered by brush in the side of a mud mound that looks like an anthill. He is glad it is not a real anthill because the stings are murderously painful. On his elbows and stomach he wriggles into the tunnel and uses a penlight to check for snakes, spiders, scorpions, and other vermin that might be in the way. He descends several yards to a small room dimly lit by a makeshift tin-can oil lamp.

Three figures greet him warmly in the semidarkness. The first is the area resistance leader, Duong Thanh Phong, whom Hiep has known for many years. Phong is middle aged, short, and slightly rounded with a reputation for solid leadership. He grew up in the same hamlet as Hiep and is like an older brother. Phong smiles at Hiep and says, "Greetings, brother, I have been telling our friends from the North about your successes against the enemy." Phong introduces the two others. Ta Quang Thinh and Nguyen Tat Thanh, both just arrived just two days ago from the North, near Hanoi.

Thinh is almost as tall as Hiep with soft black hair, cut short. Long arms that end with large, strong hands emphasize his thin face and frame. Thanh is shorter than both Hiep and Thinh, more average in height and frame, with a broad face, eyes set wide, with a high forehead topped by black hair parted and swept over smoothly. He smiles in a friendly way.

Hiep reaches out to shake their hands and says, "Welcome friends."

Thinh replies, "We are happy to be here. We are very grateful for the rice and fish you sent to restore our strength after the long journey."

Thanh adds, "Yes and we are eager to start our assignment in the South spreading word from Hanoi. We will renew resistance against the Saigon puppets."

Thinh looks at Hiep with a respectful gaze and says, "We have heard good things about your efforts here. We are eager to hear more about your good deeds."

Hiep says, "Thank you, my friends."

Taking a seat on crates with the others, Thanh looks approvingly at Phong and Hiep, then says, "Both of you have distinguished yourselves. We know you led a successful resistance when eight thousand of the enemy searched this area for tunnels during the government's Operation Crimp in 1966."

"Thank you," says Phong in a soft tone while Hiep smiles and nods his head.

Thanh contiues. "Your tactics inspired others in the Iron Triangle when the invaders came through again the next year with thirty thousand troops to destroy our tunnels, what they called Operation Cedar Falls. They had some success but we still prevailed. If it weren't for that Captain MacGregor they wouldn't have done much damage."

"Yes, he was a problem," says Phong

"A big problem," echoes Hiep. "Those Australians had the courage to go deeper into the tunnels. They found radios, medical supplies, and ammunition. They even found our district headquarters and captured our valuable maps and records. But we are back now."

"You are right," says Thinh. "The tunnels helped us to stage our great offensive during Tet in 1968. If only the local population had risen against the government, Tet would have turned out better."

Thanh adds, "At least we were more successful in the American media. Tet showed the Americans there was no truth to their government's talk of victory. Their war protests increased. That is good for us."

Thinh nods, "The next time we launch a large-scale attack we want more support from the local population. That is why we are here. We must build loyalty and increase the resistance against the puppet government and the American invaders."

Phong smiles and says, "Yes, it is true. We must gain more support from the people. We can help you do that here in the south. But please, tell us more about yourselves and how you became cadre."

Thanh draws a breath and begins, "I grew up in a rural village outside of Hanoi. My father is a teacher at the local school. He was widely known among the Vietminh for speaking about independence and freedom during the occupation of the French imperialists. This inspired me as I grew up so I volunteered to serve before my date of conscription. My enthusiasm led to my selection for the cadre."

Thinh speaks up. "That is a very similar path to mine. I grew up in a different village but had an uncle who fought against the French with the Vietminh for many years. He was a sergeant at Dien Bien Phu in 1954 under General Giap. My uncle was inspired by the speeches of Uncle Ho and his call for independence, much like the American Declaration of Independence. Also, he hated the way the French acted superior to the Vietnamese and kept them in poverty while they lived in high style. My uncle told me stories about how Diem took over the south without the elections promised by the Geneva Convention. That made me angry for revenge. I wanted to do something. So, I too joined before my conscription."

Thanh adds. "I think our backgrounds are important. We are both very motivated by the inspiration of our families and the ideals of Uncle Ho."

Gesturing with an open, right hand, Thinh says, "Yes, I agree. We both started with the usual four-month basic training camp, in the same class. The cadre instructors quickly noticed our devotion to the cause. They encouraged us and gave us extra attention."

While Thinh speaks, Thanh pictures their training as soldiers. Along with dozens of other regular soldiers they were in the Luong Son Mountains carrying packs filled with stones and sand to build strength. They trudged over the rough terrain for weeks practicing advanced infantry training in guerilla tactics with occasional breaks for instruction in political doctrine. He and Thinh often won approving words from the training cadre. They were rewarded with further political and leadership training and promoted to noncommissioned officers. Before this present assignment they attended several weeks of classes to study the methods of the enemy, the ARVN, and practice ways to influence the local South Vietnamese people.

Thinh looks over at Thanh, who had been nodding his head in agreement, and gestures with his eyes, indicating that he should share in telling. Phong and Hiep smile at that gesture and turned to look at Thanh.

Thanh sits up straight and says, "The cadre leaders said we could prove ourselves in a most useful way. We would be considered for promotion to officer rank if we performed our assignment well. They gave us the mission to go south to develop the military efforts and motivate the resistance of the local population around Ben Tre. They said, after all, Ben Tre was notable in the start of the National Liberation front back in 1960. Now we will arouse villagers' hatred of the American imperialists, point out the unfair methods of the government, and explain the better approach of our Communist Party, especially land reform for the poor."

Hiep leans back a bit, looks at both of the northerners and says, "You have done well my new friends. I am very pleased that I have been selected to accompany you on the mission to Ben Tre."

Phuong adds, "Yes, it is an honor to meet you. You will find that Hiep is one of our best young leaders in this area. Our district officers have recognized his efforts and he has been given advanced training for your mission. Also, he has visited relatives in the Ben Tre area so his knowledge of the terrain and the people will be invaluable."

"Ah good," says Than. "We could not ask for more."

With a positive ring in his voice Phong says, "Good, my friends. Now you must tell us about your journey along the trail."

Hiep leans forward, eagerly anticipating every word about the Duong Truong Son, what the Americans called the Ho Chi Minh Trail. To him, it is a legend, almost a living thing, made so by thousands of patriots toiling and struggling, carrying military supplies, soldiers marching, to overcome imperialist powers invading the homeland.

Thinh begins, "We started in trucks carrying about ten men each under a canvas roof. Normally we traveled at night and rested by day when the trucks were covered with brush and branches to camouflage them from the American aircraft. Passing through Hanoi one night we saw only a few lights because of the need to conserve electricity and to shade light from possible American air attacks."

"Yuh," says Thanh quietly, conveying that he remembers the experience.

Thinh continues, "When the trail was mostly foot-paths, it would take six months to go south. Thanks to thousands of workers it is now a web of roads, river routes, and pathways so it can be done in only six weeks. But, as specially appointed cadre, we were instructed to take longer, three months, to stop at base camps to learn the local operations. We also gave talks about the importance of our cause to the freedom fighters at the base camps."

Phong and Hiep listen intently to their new friends, eyes wide open. They adjust occasionally to the hard seats on small munitions crates. The crates had probably been carried over the trail to supply war efforts in this area, thinks Phong.

Phong says, "I hear that the Truong Son Trail is over one thousand kilometers long and that many brave and determined patriots have traveled on it, even sacrificed their lives."

Thinh nods his head and says, "It is a three-thousand-kilometer web of roads, paths, and river routes going through the Mu Gia pass in the Truong Son Mountains, its namesake, then through Laos and Cambodia. There are alternative routes in case of bombing by the Americans so we can almost always keep supplies moving, except it is much more difficult in the rainy season because of the mud. We even have an oil pipeline from the port of Vinh to the A Shau Valley area. Between way stations drivers switch and only do that part of the road they know well enough to do in the dark."

When Thinh pauses to take a breath, Thanh adds, "There are underground bases where soldiers can rest. And, we have over fifteen hundred antiaircraft guns to fight off the American planes. The trail is so good that for Tet in 1968 over 200,000 troops came down the trail. Many tons of food, fuel, and ammunition are floated in steel drums down the Bang Fai River to be caught in nets and booms and retrieved for delivery to our southern brothers."

"Going on the trail sounds like an interesting journey and much easier than the old days," says Phong.

Thanh chuckles and replies, "Well, my friend, it is not always so easy. We must contend with the American airplanes; the B-52 bombs shake the earth so that you think it is the end of the world, and the craters need to be refilled by the workers. Many people suffer from fear, boredom, and homesickness. It is not just the bombers and the hard work, but wild tigers and bears also can attack us. And even worse are the mosquitoes."

Thanh pauses for a moment, shifts his eyes around as if recalling the flying, buzzing mosquitoes, and then looks at Phong and Hiep who are both leaning forward to hear every word. "The mosquitoes were everywhere," he says softly with a sweeping wave of his hands. "We lose one in ten travelers to malaria. We were told that a good cure is to eat a worm. We were so sick that we ate the worm. Who knows if it helped, but many of us felt better."

Clearing his throat to make a gentle interruption, Thinh says, "Many of the areas had been hit by B-52 bombs repeatedly. The trees were knocked down or blown apart so it was like a wasteland. In places the roads were so bad that we had to continue on foot. There were guides to take us along the trail where we saw many volunteers working to clear the pathway and repair the damage done by bombs. Each guide would pass us off to another guide about every seven kilometers."

Phong says, "I am amazed at the perseverance and capabilities of our brothers to the north. Why do so many thousands of dan cong, especially the porters and laborers, want to work on the trail?

Thinh replies, "The answer is simple. They are fed better. They get 700 grams of rice, but back in their village their rations consist of only 450 grams of rice mixed with potatoes or corn. Eating rice on the trail is better than the extreme poverty in their villages."

"Oh," says Phong, "I see. We are fortunate in the south to be near the great rice bowl of the Mekong Delta."

Thanh picks up the story. "Cooking had to be done very carefully so it would not make smoke that could be seen by enemy aircraft. A stovepipe was used to carry the smoke away to a pile of leaves that would filter it.

Extra care was taken not to dry clothes in open places. A mistake could draw helicopters and airplanes with bombs."

The pace of the story winds down. Thanh sighs wearily and says, "Sometimes there was little rice so we would eat cassava, crayfish, rodents, or whatever else we could find. So you can see why we are happy to be here with you at this strong point before we go on."

"And we are glad you are here, my friends," says Phong.

As Hiep and Phong make a move to get up, Thanh says, "Thank you for your kindness. Before you leave, please tell us something about these tunnels here at Cu Chi. I will rest more easily if I know about my surroundings."

"Ah yes," says Hiep. We have been so eager to hear about your journey that we have neglected to explain the tunnels. Sorry."

Phong nods with a sheepish smile and says, "These tunnels were started back in the 1940s to aid us in our fight against the French. Now the entire complex stretches over 250 kilometers to link together support bases from Cambodia to the northwest of Saigon. People dig three feet of tunnel per day. We have entire villages underground, and there are schools, public spaces, hospitals, and theaters. Many places have several levels underground. Some tunnels actually run under American bases. The Americans get quite confused and alarmed when one of our fighters pops up and kills one of them right in the middle of their strongly defended areas."

"Yes," says Hiep. "We have many safe places right under the nose of the enemy. Rest assured that you could escape easily if there is a need. The bunk room below has passageways to other tunnels and exits."

Thinh says appreciatively, "These tunnels are amazing. It is thrilling to know that we are hidden near enemy bases. Like the Truong Son, the tunnels are a tremendous resource for our movement. With assets like these our victory is inevitable."

Phong gets up to show the weary guests the sleeping quarters and escape tunnels.

Hiep says, "Sleep well, my friends. I will return in a few days so we can make plans for our mission in the South."

Four

BEN TRE

The roaring and rattling engines shake everything on the plane, including my web seat in the cargo bay. The pilots must not be bothered by it too much with their radio earpieces on. It is one of those planes that has a raised tail with a ramp that can be let down to move cargo out fast. I think it is a De Havilland Caribou, a slow, two-engine prop job that is very maneuverable. It works well to make hops around the country and to set down a payload on a short runway surrounded by jungle. That fits my idea of where we are going. It is not a smooth ride so I want to get to my assignment in Ben Tre as soon as possible.

This plane ride is taking me to Ben Tre from the Mekong Delta MACV headquarters in Can Tho where I was for a few days of in-processing. While there, I learned that Ben Tre, the capitol of Kien Hoa Province, is a town the VC would like to take back. There have been several uprisings and it was hit hard during the

TET offensive in 1968. Looks like I'm headed for a hot spot. More encouraging was a briefing for about a dozen of us new advisors given by John Paul Vann, one of the top leaders of our war effort. He talked about the need "...to put a man with a rifle behind every tree to defend South Vietnam." All this processing and briefing was a lot of learning and a lot of waiting for my next move. At least waiting for an assignment is more comfortable than being in the boonies, my ultimate destination.

Before Can Tho, I had been at Di An, north of Saigon, for a couple of weeks attending an in-country school for military advisors. They taught Vietnamese language, customs, and all about the weapons we are giving to the regional forces, popular forces and village-hamlet self-defense forces. A lot of the weapons are old style, left over from WWII, like M1 rifles, M-1 and M2 carbines, Thompson submachine guns, Browning automatic rifles, and .45 caliber pistols. We also had to sharpen up on more current hardware like the M14 rifle, the .50-caliber heavy machine gun, and the M16 rifle. Basically, we have to be able to adjust to whatever equipment our Vietnamese allies might have.

While I'm sitting in this plane, thinking about all my comings and goings in this country in less than a month, it seems everyone has a reason to be somewhere else. Some grunts get bored sitting in a base camp. Maybe they want to go out into the boonies to relieve their boredom. If they are in the boonies, they want to get back to base. More realistically, they want to go to the base club where they can drink themselves into visions of a far away place. Or maybe they smoke some weed or pop a pill to escape. Even when they are lying in their hooch they crave their mail to take their minds off here and dream of somewhere else. Maybe they are thinking of home or maybe it's R&R. Anywhere but where you are.

Best dream of all is the freedom bird home. It's a constant theme. Guys tell you to the exact day when they will go home. The standard tour of duty is 365 days. Newbies get here and they know they have to endure and survive 365 days, every hour, every minute, every second. Everyone knows that it only takes one bad, ripping, explosive second to ruin your whole day, your whole life and wind up in a body bag. The old timers are the ones who are getting "short." They have counted down every single day, crossed it off a calendar, or some handcrafted, artistically decorated chart or carving. If you return from a mission after a few days, then one of the big satisfactions is that you can pull out your short-timer's chart and cross off more days to catch up.

There is a kind of seniority you get if you are a short timer. You have been so many days without getting zapped or you are only so many days from going home, and there is a certain mystique to that. A short timer inspires a sort of awe that the newbies feel when wondering how they will ever survive each and every day, realizing that the short timers will be on their way home, in fact, back in the world before they are, if ever.

Sometimes I get annoyed with the incessant chatter about being short, especially when a soldier gets a "short-timer's attitude." These guys don't want to do anything that gets them off track for home. They don't volunteer; they resist doing anything but the absolute minimum. They figure that they can get away with slacking because they will be gone by the time anyone catches up with them. The humorous side of it is all the cracks and jokes. "I'm so short I can play handball off the curb." "I'm so short I don't have time to hit the latrine." "I'm so short I can't wait in the chow line." "I'm so short I look up at the ants." "I'm so short I almost got run over by an ant while I was playing handball off the curb." "I'm so short, blah, blah, blah."

I hear most of this stuff from men assigned to duty on big, well-protected bases where I have been since being in country. Some of them act big and talk tough, but you wonder how tough they really are. Troops in the field call them REMFS, short for Rear Echelon Mother F---ers. The few guys I have met who have been out in the boonies or in combat say different things. They say, "I'm getting short but I'm afraid I won't make it" or "I'm afraid I'll get blown away before going home." These combat guys know they can be just a few days away from a freedom bird, and the only good way out is a medevac with that "red badge of courage," or enough incredible luck to finish their tour of duty in one piece. Real soon I am going to find out the difference between the REMFS and the field troops, because I am going out, way out.

We are flying over a flat landscape of endless rice paddies separated by patches of jungle and a network of waterways. Sometimes the jungle expanses are pretty extensive going from one canal or stream to the next. We are flying low enough that I can see sampans and larger, junk-type boats on the muddy water. The engines change their pitch and I realize that we are heading down. The airstrip is a dry mud track in a field with a few outbuildings on the edge. We get closer and I see that all but one of the metal shacks are Conex containers, the large shipping bins used for storage. The plane takes a quick dive, lands lightly on the airstrip and pulls up in a short distance. I realize that these birds do very well flying into tight spots, a good choice for here.

A two-and–a -half ton truck, know as a deuce-and-a-half, or deuce, pulls up. It is covered by a light layer of dust, and the standard canvass cover for the bed is off. Sand bags line the sides and bottom of the bed, making a kind of mobile foxhole in case of attack.

An E-7, sergeant first class, jumps down from behind the wheel. He is middle height, with a roman nose, and moves his stocky frame with ease. His wide waist makes him appear he's the beneficiary of regular attendance in the bar room or the mess hall. Noting my recently acquired, subdued, black First Lieutenant Bars, he says, "Welcome to Kien Hoa, lieutenant. I'm Sergeant First Class Fowler. I run the strip here."

He nods his head toward the metal shack with antennas sticking up that serves as the control tower.

He says, "You can get a ride with me to the headquarters compound. If you don't mind riding shotgun in the back, you can provide security with your M16."

I say, "Sure, sarge," thinking I have finally arrived someplace where things are happening.

With the help of Specialist Chovinowski, Sergeant Fowler's regular shotgun rider, we load a dozen cases of ammo and even more cases of C-rations into the truck from the Caribou.

Sergeant Fowler pauses before getting behind the steering wheel and says, "It's pretty safe around here, sir, but you never know when things can get hot. I'm sorry to say that yesterday we laid out eight Navy Seals in body bags for the plane to pick up."

I'm thinking, I'm coming in and eight good men went out dead; this is a nasty place. How can that even happen? Seals are some of the best trained, most qualified fighters in the service.

Sergeant Fowler sees the look on my face and says, "It must have been pretty bad because those Seals are a tough bunch, but they got ambushed on a night operation. There are some nasty spots in this province, so watch out."

"Thanks," I say with a slight catch in my voice.

I climb onto the back of the deuce and Specialist Chovinowski has already assumed a security stance, with his M16 pointing over the top of the cab. His short body is a blessing now since the sandbags cover more of him than average. I nod, and a tight smile forms on his wide face.

He says, "It should be all right this time of day."

My thoughts drift back to the Navy Seals. They probably unloaded them from this truck. Now they will be flown home for a funeral surrounded by their shocked and grieving families. I wonder if I will be going out the same way in a few weeks. A 365-day tour of duty seems like a long time when you are trying to stay alive every second of that time. That's a lot of seconds, a lot of time for bullets to fly. The truck lurches forward. There is no time to dwell on these thoughts. My eyes are wide open, scanning the front and sides and my rifle is ready, my thumb poised to flick off the safety.

When we reach Ben Tre, I see province headquarters is a set of concrete buildings surrounded by a masonry wall, located off the main street at the edge of town. It is located next to a muddy river that is several football fields across. After checking in, the admin captain says to take my gear down the road to the officers' quarters and come back later for orientation. Another lieutenant in transition, Randy Bennett, escorts me down the street past several battered French-built office buildings with porticos and shutters. He tells me these buildings are the province headquarters for the Vietnamese military and civilian government offices.

It looks like there was an intense exchange of weapons fire here. Somebody had a quarrel with the government. The shutters are pocked with bullet holes. Ding marks show where automatic weapons fire struck the walls. Randy mentions that a highly placed VC leader, Madame Nguyen Thi Dinh, is from this province, so maybe that gave the VC an incentive to attack so fiercely. This jogs my memory.

I say, "Isn't Ben Tre the town that was in the news, you know...they had to destroy it to save it?"

Randy shakes his head affirmatively and says, "Yeah, I remember that. It was the brave men of the 3/39th in the Ninth Infantry Division who fought here door-to-door in 1968, TET. Those guys were tough. Still, they couldn't get the VC out without shelling and bombing the town."

I say, "We're lucky those guys went before us. It looks pretty safe now."

We arrive at the transient officers quarters. It is a small, old French hotel of two stories, made of concrete, surrounded by a low wall with a metal gate. A guardhouse flanks the gate. There is a Vietnamese guard outside, armed with a WWII-vintage M2 carbine, a thirty round banana clip sticking out of the bottom. He smiles and nods.

I say, "Chao," and smile back.

I am thinking that this is pretty slim security and am glad that I am going to have my M16 with me. I wonder if a bandolier of seven twenty-round magazines is enough.

Downstairs is a large lounge with a bar in the back corner. Over the front door hangs a captured AK-47. At the top of the stairs is a long hall leading to a back window overlooking a muddy canal or creek. Bamboo and thatch huts line the banks. Rickety looking outhouses stand out over the water. Palm trees line the riverbank between the houses. Here and there a palm frond or a coconut floats in the water and is taken by the slow current down the stream to the larger river. Randy tells me to find a spot upstairs in a large room with a couple of army bunks.

He says, "See ya later. Gotta go back and do some paperwork."

"Yeah, thanks Randy," I say.

There is a large patio off the room. It overlooks the street and is rimmed with a waist-high cement wall. Automatically I think it would afford some protection in the event of a firefight. I do not think there will be an attack on the rear of the hotel because the steep wall is right over the riverbank and it would be difficult to climb, especially under defensive fire.

Standing on the patio, I imagine a squad of VC in black pajamas down in the street trying to shoot their way into the gate past the guard. I see myself returning fire with single, aimed shots to conserve ammunition. There is no telling how long it would take for reinforcements to arrive, if they ever do. This mental picture is pushed away by the realization that the VC would probably not find it worthwhile to attack an old hotel with a low priority target like me, especially if they had to waste precious ammunition to shoot their way in.

The next morning I am sitting in the lounge downstairs writing letters home. Suddenly, I hear three explosions out back. I run upstairs and grab my M16 and rush down the hall to the back window. There are no more booms so I peer cautiously out the window. There is no damage to the hotel but a small tree has been blown up. Apparently the VC sent a few rockets or mortars my way but they only landed harmlessly on the riverbank. I later learn that it is a regular practice of the VC to fire a few rounds at the several military facilities to harass and disrupt the headquarters and possibly hit a target. For the moment, I am glad the hotel has thick walls and that VC rockets are not that easy to aim.

The admin officer says that I will have to wait until tomorrow to get assigned to a MAT team, but to be ready to move out. It gives me a chance to go to the province compound mess hall, which has good American chow prepared by Vietnamese cooks. I eat a hearty breakfast of bacon, eggs and fried potatoes, just like home, because I don't know how many good meals are in my future. I look forward to lunch because a guy next to me in the mess says they have good burgers and potato salad. It is amazing how we have good home cooking in the middle of rice paddies, coconut trees, canal fish, south east Asian culture and a shooting war thanks to the military supply system.

After the highlight of the mess hall the rest of the day is pretty slow. No one really has time to talk to a newbie like me, so I spend time collecting my thoughts, writing in my journal and finishing a letter to Cathy. I long to talk to her in person. Not just to see her pretty brown eyes, sandy brown hair and sweet smile, but to hear the details of our baby daughter's antics, and really talk about our lives. I would like to hear her opinion on my growing concerns about this war. Our letters, as numerous as they are, just can't replace being together face to face. She is my trusted confidant. A year away from each other is a big chunk out of our lives.

I also spend time playing board games with the other newbie, Randy Bennett. He is a ring knocker graduate of West Point, even has the big ring, but he seems like a regular guy. That's important to me, with a ROTC commission, since the prevailing wisdom is that West Pointers only respect fellow academy grads. He grew up in New Jersey, and I grew up in New York so we have some things in common and get along fine.

In the late afternoon I go sit on the rooftop patio in one of those woven plastic bucket chairs that can be found in the local market. I light up a panatela cigar to savor the moment. My new Zippo lighter works great. I just bought it at the closet-like PX in the compound. That's where they sell booze, cigars, cigarettes, canned goods that taste better than C-rations, and whatever else they can cram in there. I never had a Zippo before, but everyone seems to have one. I like the metallic click that it makes when opened, and the way it makes an instant flame with an abrasive flick of the steel flintwheel. I flick it a few times just to hear the scratch of the flint and see the flame jump from the windscreen, and then hear the snap of the closing lid that extinguishes the flame. Maybe I should have had it engraved, but I think that any markings would help the enemy if I were captured.

The cigar is a pleasant vice. I know that it is probably not healthy to smoke too many of them, but, hey, what's a little self-destruction when Victor Charles would be happy to end my bad habits for good? Besides,

I probably have a self-destructive streak in me. I always liked riding motorcycles, and I rolled my car a few years ago. I have always liked some new adventure. That might have something to do with how I wound up in Nam. Who knows? Now that things are deadly serious, I resolve to reflect more on what is happening around me.

Sitting in the hotel and smoking the stogie is a quiet moment between events, a pause to ponder my circumstances and to relish being alive in the Nam. I think how strange it is for me to have a respite, in the middle of conflict going on all around me. I am stuck in an administrative process while there are men in the jungle bent on killing each other. The eight dead Navy Seals are testament to that. Not far from me are night ambushes, rocket attacks, snipers, and booby traps. I am impatient to get to my assignment but glad to have one more day of relative calm.

I think of the chain of events that brought me here. Why am I here? Many of my generation decided to go to Canada or jail instead of going to Vietnam. It can't all be cowardice. It takes a certain amount of courage to act on principle or to stand up for a belief. After all, that's what our founding fathers did. If dissenters are truly driven by conscience, then I respect them, but not loudmouth groupies who are more concerned with saving their own skins than honest civil disobedience. A man in my situation is faced with duty, jail, flight, or the luck of a high draft number. I choose duty in the hope that my leaders are better informed and wiser than I am.

The more I learn about this country and the history of our involvement, the more unsettling it is. I have growing doubts and even question the sanity of being here. Yes, I am a young man doing his duty, a value that is ingrained in me. I was a Boy Scout. My family has served. I believe a citizen should earn the rights afforded by their country. My country called me to war. My personal conviction to serve is strong, yet I am conflicted by the surging contradictions around me.

I came here on the faith that the leaders of my country would only send young men to fight and die for a worthwhile cause. But our politicians disagree. Why couldn't they figure it out before getting into this mess? This war is too long. Sun Tzu, the Chinese warrior who wrote *The Art of War*, knew that wars have to be won quickly to avoid failure. Something is wrong.

In contrast to the growing war protests back home, it was somewhat encouraging to hear J.P. Vann speak to us new advisors while down in Can Tho. He gave a seemingly sincere speech about stopping the spread of communism and keeping the dominoes from falling in Southeast Asia. He was inspiring and convincing. He still believes, so why do others doubt?

One thing that appeals to my sense of justice is the stories about the atrocities committed by Ho's regime. These stories make me want to help protect the innocent.

Back in 1956, according to one story, Ho's troops slaughtered about six thousand unarmed villagers in An province to quell a tax revolt. His strong-arm squads forced confessions from North Vietnamese landowners, civic leaders, schoolteachers, and other potential, contrary thought leaders. Confessions were often followed by mock trials, and then the convicted were shot, beheaded, or beaten to death.

I also heard that in addition to other crimes against humanity, Ho's followers attacked the educational system in South Vietnam to suppress the independent thinking of an educated populace. Teachers who refused to comply with VC demands were shot, beheaded, or had their throats cut. When children refused VC demands to quit school the fingers of one six-year-old girl were cut off in front of other children to threaten them further.

Amid all this turmoil, it seems to me that the average Vietnamese would just like to lead a peaceful life and be done with all the conflict. I imagine they want to farm their land, conduct their business, and not worry about their children stepping on booby traps, or their families being tortured or killed because of competing allegiances and retribution from whoever is in control of their village at the time.

At this point in the game, this war seems hopeless and useless and probably should have been avoided in the first place. If this isn't hell, it sure is a good substitute.

It really doesn't matter what I think because I'm in it now. It just comes down to staying alive and doing my best with the others who are in this too. It's do or die, even if you are asking questions why.

My mind is filled with this confusion and I don't have time to sort it all out. All I can do is stuff it down and be strong. A crazy stream of words about military mistakes marches through my head. I jot them down in my journal, almost like verses, as if capturing them will help anchor my thoughts:

Remember the Persian defeat at Salamis,
Remember the Roman defeat at Edessa,
And Napoleon's failed invasion of Russia.
Remember the devastation at Gallipoli,
And Remember the Little Big Horn too.
But hail all the brave soldiers, who fight
With the valor of the Light Brigade.
And huzzah for Pete Seeger, also
Peter, Paul, and Mary who ask
If we will ever, ever, really learn.
Onward to graveyards, onward to graveyards,
Will we ever learn? Will we ever learn?
Oh, never, never will we ever learn.

Five

FIREBASE BRAVO

The next day I am on a chopper headed toward the South China Sea to join Mobile Advisory Team (MAT) 23 on Vietnamese Firebase Bravo. They are located on the base with a Vietnamese unit of artillery operating two pairs of 105-millimeter howitzers, the salvation of infantry units under attack. The base also has a company of Vietnamese regional force infantry to protect the artillery and conduct operations in the area. The outpost is on the outskirts of Thanh Phu District, about forty five kilometers, known as klicks to us military people, southeast of Ben Tre, near the South China Sea.

Huey pilots like to come in fast and low, just over the treetops, to make it hard for VC gunners to get a bead on them. The pilot today is no exception. Most of the ride is at 1500 feet with the pilot and copilot following a bearing to our destination. I sit in the back seat with the mailbags and supplies of food and ammo. The door gunner follows the terrain with his eyes and the barrel of his M60 machine gun. He is ready to fire, but there is no need right now.

We must be near our destination. I can see the South China Sea on the horizon. The pilot calls MAT 23 on the radio and asks if there has been any enemy contact within the last twenty-four hours. They answer in the affirmative but say there is no contact now and all is clear for a landing. They will hold artillery fire and pop a smoke grenade to mark the Lima Zulu or landing zone. The chopper swings wide past the triangular, French style, mud-walled artillery base staying high above the surrounding jungle that is a few hundred yards from the fort. I consider the possibility that an AK-47 round might rip through the floor of the chopper and sting my butt. It makes me squirm in my seat.

The chopper flies out over the South China Sea and then drops to a height only one hundred feet above the waves. I relax with the thought that there are no VC gunners in the water and enjoy the exhilaration of flying so low. These pilots must love any excuse to have a little fun. The rush of the chopper just over the shimmering sea is breathtaking. The beauty of the water against the sandy beach with a backdrop of jungle green looks like something out of a travel brochure.

I bring my mind back into focus and hear the pilot say into the radio, "Two Six, I see yellow smoke."

A voice responds, "This is Two Six, that is affirmative."

The chopper races over the tree tops toward the smoke and in a minute we are hovering over a makeshift steel-grate-and-mud landing pad just outside the fort. As we set down, the gunner signals for me to move out, and he hands supplies out to the waiting handful of men in US uniforms.

With the roar of the chopper blades and the whirl of dust, I jump out of the chopper with my gear and follow the others to the gate, making sure to avoid the tail rotor, known to take the heads off careless soldiers. The chopper lifts off and is out of there after less than thirty seconds on the ground. Less time to become a target for a long-range rifle shot from the tree line.

A tall, strongly built man at the gate with captain's insignia on a US uniform sticks out his hand and says, "Welcome Lieutenant Van Howe, we've been expecting you. My name is John Blake, team leader, and these are," he gestures with his hand toward the two E-7 sergeants bringing in the mail bag and supplies, "Sergeant Clarkson and Sergeant Bradford."

The sergeants give me a nod as they walk past. Captain Blake says, "Let's get inside and we'll talk." The two sergeants first class walk toward a large shed. SFC Clarkson is stocky with a middle aged rounding of the shoulders and a ruddy complexion and reddish hair. SFC Bradford is younger, taller, almost my 6 foot height, with a strong, lean frame and brown hair blending into the tan on his thin face.

We enter the twelve-foot by twenty-foot plywood building with a tin roof and a half wall of screen. The sides and roof are covered with a double layer of sand-bags. Inside it looks like a small vacation cabin without any amenities, more like a garden shed filled with olive drab cots, footlockers, tables, radios, ammunition bandoliers hanging from nails on the wall, an M79 grenade launcher hanging by its strap on a hook, the black metallic and plastic of M16s standing against the wall, and cardboard boxes of C-rations and other gear. On one side there is a propane refrigerator and stove. Empty wooden ammo boxes are pulled around the two folding field tables.

"It looks like luxury to me; how did you get this house here?" I say.

Captain Blake says, "They flew in the prefab pieces on a Chinook and we put it together."

"Nice work, pretty comfy." I say this, knowing that the accommodations could be a lot worse.

The shed even offers a wooden floor over the mud surrounding it.

Besides Blake, myself, Bradford, and Clarkson, there are two other men in the hut. One is a staff sergeant medic, a confident looking black man of medium build with a slight belly bulge under his t-shirt who smiles broadly from his seat while sorting through a medical bag. The other is a sturdy looking, round faced Vietnamese sergeant, smaller than the rest of us, giving me an inquiring look.

"This is Doc Jackson, our medic, and Trung Si Sang, our interpreter," says Captain Blake.

He looks at them and says, "With Lieutenant Van Howe here, we a have a full team."

I shake hands with them and say, "Good to meet you."

Sergeant Bradford steps up to shake my hand and says, "Call me Brad for short."

"And everybody calls me Clarkee," says Sergeant Clarkson with a handshake.

Captain Blake says, "I'm glad you're here because it's difficult to rotate anyone back for R&R or supplies when we're short handed, and we just lost Lieutenant Lane."

"What happened?" I say.

"Oh he got a psychological evac, poor sucker."

"Huh?"

"Yep," says Blake. "He went out on patrol around the base here about a week after he arrived. He was with Clarkee and a platoon of our RFs, what we call the regional forces."

Sergeant Clarkson who is sitting at the table with us nods his head and says, "Yeah." His round face contorts into a flat-lipped grimace.

Blake continues, "They went out across the field in front of the base and...you tell it Clarkee, since you were there."

Sergeant Clarkson picks up the story. "We got to the edge of the jungle where there is a stream, more like a muddy canal, with one of those rickety bamboo bridges over it. Well, the RFs stopped short of the bridge and got down and waited to see if there was any enemy activity across the stream, back in the jungle. After a few minutes one squad got up and went across the bridge. We all held our breath to see if they would take fire. You see, there are VC all around here. Then Lieutenant Lane said he is not going over the bridge. He said it is too risky. Our squad had already crossed over and was securing the other side, but he said that they might stir up the VC and bullets would be flying. He made a good point, but the squad on the other side was taking no rounds. Maybe the VC could have fired a rocket or a mortar at us but for a combat zone it looked pretty safe to me. I was anxious to get across fast before anything did break loose, but the lieutenant just kind of froze up. Something just came over him. So, I just figured the best thing was to get him back up the hill to the base. He came along with me, but he was sort of in a daze."

Captain Blake adds, "After a night in his bunk he seemed normal but kind of remote. I asked him what happened and he just said pretty much what Clarkee said. By that time the RF company commander asked if he was OK. I figured he wasn't going to work out so I sent him to Major Grady, our district chief, on the next chopper. The major confirmed my sense that he was more of a liability than a help. Last thing I heard he had a desk job in Saigon. I guess the brass figured they could be kind to him with all the craziness of this war. He will probably make it through and go home, get an honorable discharge, and become some rich executive."

I'm thinking to myself that Lane is getting an easy ride. He didn't even have a red badge of courage. He was awarded an olive drab cover-up. I know that Lane probably didn't have any control over his behavior, or at least never learned how to deal with freezing fear. He just couldn't take it. In the back of my mind I remember the guy that General Patton slapped. Back then there were no excuses, just do or die. You held your shield or came back on it. Here things are a bit more gray. There is conflict over what we are doing here, there is too much confusion, there are too many excuses, and too many things that don't make sense.

So, if you have courage and discipline and do your duty then you are rewarded with life in a mud hole, a chance to dodge enemy fire, and the privilege of possible injury or death. If you can't hack it you get a desk job, officers' clubs, and a free ride home. But the little voice inside me says there is no honor in that. I hope I can do better than that. I want to do better than that, dumb cluck that I am. After telling the story about Lieutenant Lane, Captain Blake is looking at me for any sign of how I will react.

Inside, I know that I am unproven in combat and maybe I too will lose my cool, but I say, "Captain Blake, I won't let you down."

"We're counting on you," he says. "You know, it isn't that simple with Lieutenant Lane. There is more to the story." Clarkson nods his head and takes a sip of his coffee. Blake lifts his chin in a gesture to Clarkson that he should tell more of the story.

Sergeant Clarkson says, "About a week before this incident we went out on an overnight patrol with a reinforced platoon of the regional forces. They had a couple extra machine gun teams and an extra squad of riflemen, about forty men in all including Lieutenant Lane and me. We were after some Victor Charlies that fired at us from the wood line out across that big field down front. Every other night they would let it rip with their automatic fire for a few minutes but not long enough for us to call in arty on top of them. We could see the muzzle blasts. If they caught one of our guys off guard they could blow his head off, but fortunately that hasn't happened yet. So, with our urging, the RF company commander decided to go out after them."

After another sip of coffee Clarkson continues, "We went out about two klicks beyond that stream or canal down there. We didn't spot Charlie, but we did find a cache of red mackerel cans that were made into explosive devices, full of C-4 and nails, glass, and such. No doubt they were aiming to use those nasty things on us. Anyway, it was getting dark, and we didn't want to walk back to the base without good visibility if Charles had a chance to set some of those explosives in our way, so we set up a night defensive perimeter."

I am thinking, good for Lieutenant Lane. He went across the bridge to hunt Charlie in the jungle. That shows some spunk.

Meanwhile, Sergeant Bradford is standing at the stove cooking up a concoction of field rations and canned goods brought in by the chopper. A spicy aroma fills the shed and I start to feel hungry. Sergeant Bradford did not go light on the hot sauce, which is pretty typical for GIs trying to doctor up the usual field chow.

"That stuff smells real good," says Clarkson.

"Thanks. This is my mama's old recipe, GI style, kinda like a GI jambalaya. Finish up your story because it will be ready in a few minutes."

Clarkson goes on, "So we have our forty men in a big circle with teams of two. The machine guns are set up to give interlocking fields of fire. The gunners put stakes in the ground to guide their fire at night. We set up some trip lines with tin cans filled with stones so they will rattle if Charles bumps them in the dark. We put out half a dozen claymores with the wires running back to fighting positions so they can be command detonated. Those claymores give a big blast and throw shrapnel out something fierce. They would cut through a squad of Charlies pretty quick."

"Anyway," says Clarkson, "things are pretty quiet for a few hours. Then one of the teams near us hears a can rattle. They duck down and blow off the claymore. The blast shatters the night and the thing shoots shrapnel right back at us. Charles must have snuck up and turned the claymore on us. Luckily, the guys near it had their heads down, but the darn thing sent shrapnel over our heads and into the back of one soldier on the other side of the perimeter. He howled with the pain, but didn't die because he was only on the edge of the blast zone and it didn't have full force. The medic shot him full of morphine and they moved him back to the command post in the center of the perimeter. Meanwhile, nothing else happens. We listen for sounds in the dark. We are careful not to fire our weapons so the muzzle flash won't give away our positions and give Charles a target. There are no more rattles, no sounds, nothing. It goes on like that for hours. After a while Lieutenant Lane and me take turns trying to get some sleep. Finally, we see the first light of dawn."

Clarkson pauses and takes a breath, "It starts to get light enough so you can see the man next to you. Then suddenly we hear a scream from the other side of the perimeter. The regional force platoon sergeant and Lieutenant Lane crouch and run over there. What they see is one soldier with a shocked look on his face, pointing at the blood soaked shirt of his buddy. His buddy was lying back with his throat slit; eyes wide open with a look of surprise on his face. Charlie just slithered up there when these guys fell asleep and slit one, left the other to freak out, and spread fear in the ranks. After a while, when the men settled down and the company commander checked it all out, we carried out dead and wounded back to the base in ponchos. On the way back we checked very carefully for mines and booby traps."

Captain Blake says, "I think this incident spooked Lieutenant Lane. He just wasn't going to go back out there."

"Yeah," I say. "I think that could put a scare in any-body. It's a nightmare. How are you dealing with it, Sergeant Clarkson, uh, Clarkee?

"I'm OK. This is my second tour and I've seen enough to get used to it."

In the back of my mind I'm thinking, when this stuff happens we are just supposed to steel up and keep on going, like soldiers and victims have been doing forever. But Lieutenant Lane was scared witless. He couldn't jam it down deep enough and it just came back and froze him up.

I have a better understanding of Lane now. At least there is a good reason for his fear. He doesn't have a red badge of courage, but he has a mental scar that could take a long time to heal. Either that or he is a cold, cal-culating coward who figured he just isn't going to take any chances. I keep my thoughts to myself, but look at Clarkson and say, "That's one heck of bad day. It could happen to anyone."

Just then, we hear the distinctive popping sound of AK-47 automatic weapons fire from the perimeter of the fort.

Blake says, "Don't worry, lieutenant, the sandbags on our roof can take a rocket"

I am thinking how nice that is as I grab my M16 and a bandolier of ammunition. A rocket hits the roof with a *whomp!* The whole shack shakes. Dust scatters from the rafters as we all dive for the floor.

Bradford yells out, "Jeez, those VC are going to ruin my stew!" He slams the lid on the pot and turns off the stove.

There are two more *whomps* outside about thirty feet away. Then, two more whomps hit farther on.

Blake says, "That's usually it, five rockets, now we get the attack."

We all run out with weapons ready to the back wall of the fort. A squad of RFs is pouring automatic rifle fire over the wall, popping up alternatively to fire a few rounds at a time in a disciplined way. We crouch behind the sandbags and can hear the bullets whizzing over our heads.

Blake says, "This is more than usual, like a heavy attack."

The bullets keep coming in short bursts from different directions. Our squad is holding out well. We join them for a few shots at the enemy, I pop up with my rifle and seeing a few bursts from the opposite jungle, fire a short burst of my own. Who knows if I hit anything since I'm not lingering over the top of the sandbags to look. More squads are covering the other walls of the fort in case of attack from a different direction.

Captain Blake says, "Our own arty is too close to get a shot, but there is a MAT team at Firebase Alpha about eight klicks north. Would you like the pleasure of calling in a few rounds on top of our visitors?"

I say, "You bet. What's Alpha's call sign?" and reach for the map in my cargo pocket.

Sergeant Bradford brings up the radio, an ANPRC 25 with a long antennae.

Blake says, "Their call sign is Foxtrot Alpha Two Niner. Yours is Showdown Three Five. They know where we are on the map."

I grab the handset on a coiled wire and key the mike: "Foxtrot Alpha Two Niner, Foxtrot Alpha Two Niner, This is Showdown Three Five, Showdown Three Five, over."

A voice cracks over the handset, "This is Foxtrot Alpha Two Niner, over"

"This is Showdown Three Five, fire Mission, target at Grid 521326, direction 6100 mils, distance 200 meters, platoon in bush. Fire one HE. Danger close. I will adjust fire, over."

"This is Foxtrot Alpha Two Niner, I copy Grid 521326, direction 6100 mils, distance 200 meters, platoon in bush, fire one High Explosive, danger close, wait to adjust, over."

"This is Showdown Three Five, that's a roger, good copy, over."

"Showdown Three Five, this is Foxtrot Alpha Two Niner, shot, over."

I reply, "Shot out." This tells them I know the round was fired.

I am thinking it would be good to drop rounds behind the target and walk them in closer. The range of a 105 howitzer round is eleven thousand meters, so we are well within range and accuracy should be fairly good. The bursting radius of a round is twenty by thirty meters and the casualty radius is 175 meters. I need to keep this in mind so I can adjust fire and not bring it in on top of us. I hear a howitzer round coming near and then it crashes into the jungle about three hundred meters from our position. There is a momentary lull in the enemy firing. I hope they are going to retreat right into my barrage. Captain Blake looks at me with an approving smile and nods.

I key the hand set again:
"Foxtrot Alpha Two Niner, This is Showdown Three Five, over"

"This is Foxtrot Alpha Two Niner, over"

"This is Showdown Three Five, correction, drop one hundred, right fifty, and fire five rounds for effect."

"This is Two Niner, Roger, drop one hundred, right fifty, and fire five rounds for effect."

"This is Three Five, roger."

There is a brief pause and, "This is Two Niner, shots over."

"Roger, shots out," I reply.

"This is Two Niner, splash over." They send this message to let me know the rounds will hit in a few seconds.

I key the mike and say, "splash out."

Like boxcars rushing through the air we hear the rounds in the air and the *THUMP, THUMP, THUMP, THUMPWAWHUMP*. Trees are blown into the air. Jungle brush and mud form clouds of debris. There is not too much dust because of all the mud. There is a pause. Everyone listens for sounds of the enemy. There is no sound.

I say: "Foxtrot Alpha Two Niner, this is Showdown Three Five, rounds on target, casualties unknown. End fire mission, over"

"This is Two Niner, casualties unknown. End fire mission, over."

This is Three Five, thank you much, out"

Sergeant Bradford says, "Good job LT, you blew them away or at least they're scared speechless and running back to momma."

"Way to go, Van," says Blake.

There are approving nods from the Vietnamese troops around us. They are happy they do not have to fight off an attack on our wall. Captain Blake says, "It's getting too late now, so a patrol will go out in the morning to check for body count."

The next day a patrol of eleven bravos, military code for infantry, goes out. There are no bodies to be found, just a North Vietnamese canteen, a couple of shreds of black pajamas, a VC helmet, the shattered stock of an AK-47 assault rifle, and jungle leaves with blood splatters. There are blood trails in the jungle. We theorize that a few attackers survived or they had a rear element that dragged the bodies off for an honorable burial.

———

The next few weeks are mostly quiet. That is, except for the artillery fire missions every day and every night. *Blam, Blam, Blam* and more *Blam!* I go out on a few patrols with the regional forces. Our team splits this duty up so just two or three of us go out while the others stay at the base to coordinate with the company commander and the artillery commander or district headquarters. Most of our patrols don't flush out any VC, but we know they are there because we find more explosives caches and actual booby traps set up to get us. Mr. Charles still takes an occasional pot shot at us from the wood line, but not as many since we rained down on their raid with artillery. I feel good that I have the sand to go across the bridge and into the jungle, but I do not want to get my throat slit. I don't want to see anyone get their throat slit, and I respect our adversaries for their cunning and skill. Mr. Charles is king of the jungle when we go back to our little mud fort, and I don't want to take a walk out there in the moonlight.

There is one day when we have a really tough incident. Sergeant Bradford and I go down the slope, across the field to our usual bridge crossing with a platoon of the regional force infantry. It is going to be a routine patrol, just go a few klicks to scare up Charles and let him know he is not welcome. Maybe we will find a few booby traps and blow them up.

We are getting ready to follow our usual procedure to cross the bridge. We spread out on the safe side with weapons pointing across the stream. The plan is to cover a squad that crosses over. That squad will secure the other side and then the rest of our force crosses. This time, just as our first squad is trying to cross over there is a hail of automatic fire from the jungle on the other side. One of our guys tumbles off the bridge and another rolls down the muddy bank. The rest of us drop to the ground and crawl for cover behind logs and humps of mud. Our guys fire rapidly on full automatic, rock and roll, so the exposed squad can crawl behind logs and trees to get cover. The enemy keeps firing with AK-47s and semiautomatic weapons, and then fires off a rocket propelled grenade, or RPG. It hits a tree and knocks off a branch.

Bullets crack and whiz through the air and spit into the mud around us. Chips of bark fly off logs and stumps. We have run into a VC hornet's nest. The enemy has the advantage of terrain—they are across the stream and we can't easily advance or retreat uphill without casualties.

I think that this could go on for a long time and we have dead or wounded to evacuate. Worse, Charles has the advantage with weapons. His heavy AK-47 rounds can penetrate the jungle foliage that camouflages him and our lighter M16 rounds can't penetrate his hiding places very well. Although the M16 is more accurate, at this close range Charles can blast away and hit us. I can also see that one of our guys has a jammed rifle, probably from dirt in the firing mechanism. Meanwhile, the bullets are flying and the RPGs give Charlie another advantage. Brad is encouraging the regional force platoon leader to keep up the defense and get ready to maneuver. I am carrying the radio on my back so I grab the handset to report our contact with the enemy. Maybe we can direct some mortar fine on them.

Luckily, I hear a call from Ishmael 11, our province supply chopper pilot. This is the same chopper that delivered me here and drops supplies every few days. By now I am familiar with his call sign and I am glad to hear him.

He says: "Showdown, Showdown, this is Ishmael One One, Ishmael One One, over."

"This is Showdown Three Five, I have you Lima Charlie (loud and clear), over"

"This is Ishmael One One, we are arriving at your position and saw an RPG flash, what is your situation?"

"This is Showdown Three Five, we are in contact with enemy and need fire support."

"This is Ishmael One One, roger, pop smoke and identify enemy position."

"Roger, smoke is out, enemy is fifty yards south across the stream."

"This is Ishmael One One, roger, copy red smoke, enemy fifty yards south across stream."

"This is Three Five, roger, good copy red smoke."

"This is One One, coming in."

The Huey comes in close over the treetops and rushes by the enemy position, machine gun blazing a hail of bullets down into the jungle. The enemy firing stops momentarily, then resumes with a little less intensity. Ishmael 11 turns the bird and comes back for another run at Charlie. He swipes them again with long bursts from the machine gun. By the third time around Charles is firing sporadically. Ishmael dwells a bit over the spot and rains down a good dose of automatic fire. With this, our second squad rushes across the bridge and secures the other side. Our third squad follows and starts maneuvering against Charles. The first squad gathers up their two fallen men and starts first aid.

I can see that both men are alive, but one is seriously wounded.

I get on the radio: "Ishmael One One, this is Showdown Three Five, thank you much. You put them down and we are securing the area, over."

"This is Ishmael One One, our pleasure, glad to give our gun a workout and give you a hand. We couldn't see them all through the trees but we may have winged a few. Do you need any further help, over?"

"This is Three Five, request you stand by for medevac, over."

"This is Ishmael One One, I copy medevac, when will you be ready?"

"This is Three Five, we can get them to the Lima Zulu in ten mikes"

"This is Ishmael One One, roger we will make supply drop at your Lima Zulu and stand by for pick up."

"This is Three Five, roger. Thank you much, out"

With that, Ishmael turns the bird and flies back to Firebase Bravo.

Our first squad takes their wounded up the hill and Ishmael picks them both up for immediate evacuation to a field hospital. Sergeant Bradford and I go with the second and third squads to clear through the VC position. We find one dead and one wounded. There are blood trails leading back into the jungle. We pursue the trails but they soon dry up and we can't catch Charles. We don't want to get too far into their territory with only two squads in case they get reinforcements or set up an ambush, so we give it up.

We carry out the dead and wounded VC. They have good intelligence value. The wounded VC has a bleeding leg and a gash on his head and looks like he will live. He may give up useful information during interrogation. Someone may recognize the dead man and that can be factored into the intelligence puzzle. We are all pretty happy that we finally contacted Charles and took a bite out of his hide without any KIA of our own.

Other than that action, about the only startling thing that happened is that an outpost in another part of Tan Phu district was overrun and the MAT team is missing. Half of the popular force platoon that they lived with was killed in a fierce fight. One of the American sergeants was found dead of bullet wounds, a forty-five pistol clutched in his hand, and several empty M16 magazines by his side. He went down fighting with guns blazing.

There was a report about American prisoners being paraded through a village on the South China Sea. Some friendly villagers reported it to district headquarters and they passed it on to us. The word is that three advisors were taken through the village, tied together with a rope, and rat cages on their heads. The rat cages were made of sticks tied together like a birdcage with a hole in the bottom so it can be placed over a head. Rats can be placed in the cage to torment the prisoner. I can imagine how frightening it would be to have your head thrust into one of the cages with furry bodies with long tails brushing or nipping your face.

When they came through the village the cages did not have any rats in them, but the prisoners had red wounds on their ears, noses, and other parts of their faces. They were bedraggled, hungry, and tired looking. They were tied to a tree while a communist cadre in black pajamas made a speech to the villagers. He said that this is what happens to American aggressors and friends of the South Vietnamese government. He warned the villagers not to side with the government forces, but to support and aid the Viet Cong freedom fighters. After the speech the prisoners were led off. Our district headquarters tells us there is an extensive search of the area that is going on right now. I hope they find them, but it is not easy because Charlie knows how to hide in the jungle. Charlie knows his home area very well.

One night, I sit outside our hooch on an ammo crate where it is safe to light up a cigar without attracting enemy fire. My trusty Zippo gives me a flame to pull into the panatela. The smoke feels good. I enjoy the small pleasure of the cigar after a long day and it helps to ward off the bugs on a still night. Tonight, though, there is a light breeze off the South China Sea that keeps the bugs away.

The image of the advisors taken prisoners stays in my mind. It is horrifying and haunts me. I don't want to be captured. I wonder if my M16 will be enough. We had a dirty one jam on us here in the heat of a firefight and there are reports of bad ammo that causes carbon fouling. The AK-47 has a reputation for reliability even if it is heavier and less sophisticated than the M16. Who cares if we can carry more of our lighter ammo if the rifle won't shoot? There is no time to clean your rifle when Charlie is trying to light you up. Failure of my only weapon is something I fear. It gives me a chill and tightens my gut. I resolve to acquire a pistol as a sidearm to give me a back up. I want to go down fighting if it comes to that. You have to do what you have to do.

Six

AP AN THANH

Four of us from MAT 23 are on the way to Ap An Thanh, a small village that is part of our Thanh Phu district. The village flanks a modest waterway with muddy banks just large enough to squeeze in a couple of water taxis and fishing boats across the width. A lone, mud sided, French style, triangular outpost with corner towers sits on a large island that forms the opposite bank from the village landing. The outpost is located there to keep the VC from coming across the island and attacking the landing, an important hub for commerce between the village and the district town three kilometers up the canal.

We are traveling in a beat up, well-worn army jeep over the dike trails leading from Firebase Bravo to An Thanh. The terrain is fairly flat and open with wide spans of rice paddies between the tree lines. We stop by the village of An Quy where our team has responsibility for another small outpost of infantry popular forces.

Unfortunately, we are there when the platoon is burying one of their own. To pay our respects we decide to stay overnight to attend the funeral and, later, inspect the outpost. We string net hammocks from poles holding up a thatched, shed roof in the corner of the mud fort, under one of the three towers used for observation and fighting. The high structure is held up on lashed and pegged poles surrounded by mud on the outside with a sandbagged nest eight or ten feet high off the ground. The nest gives an elevated view of the flat terrain so the guards can fire down on an attacking enemy, somewhat like the defenders of old medieval castles from their high towers.

The funeral takes place in the village burial ground near the fort. The bare pine-plank coffin is born by an honor guard of soldiers, still in their fatigues, carrying their rifles on slings. The mother, wife, other family, and friends of the fallen young man grieve in discordant cries and wails while following the brief procession. After the coffin is lowered into the ground, the honor guards stand aside and, in the usual ritual of the popular forces, point the muzzles of their M16 rifles up toward the sky and fire bursts of bullets on full automatic. The rattling cacophony seems to ward off evil, relieve the fullness of grief, and send the deceased onward to ancestors with a fanfare. Nonetheless, the automatic rifle fire makes me worry where the hail of bullets will land. I stop holding my breath and give a shallow sigh of relief when, miraculously, there are no casualties from this display of firepower.

The next day, we assure the platoon leader we care about his unit and a quick review shows us that his platoon is capable of keeping An Quy secure. The sun is still not halfway up in the sky when we head out to the next outpost that is on the way to An Thanh.

The jeep dodges water buffaloes, chickens, and ditches as we pass by small homesteads with farmers drying out their shrimp catch or thrashing their rice. In some spots the trail is barely passable because of mud ditches and high water. Months ago the jeep was flown in by Chinook because the trails were impassible. It has been used like a mule to haul gear, ammunition for howitzers, and building materials for bunkers. It is missing seat cushions, but that is actually an advantage since it leaves us room to stack sandbags on the bottom of the floor and seat frames. These give us some small comfort against the possibility of running over a land mine that will blow us off the road, leaving us mangled in a ditch and probably ruining our day. With the protection of the sandbags, maybe one of us would survive to call in a medevac.

When we use the jeep, it shows the farmers that the government is able to travel in the area once dominated by the VC. It also gives us the ability to move more swiftly than on foot before the VC can organize an ambush. Plus we can save our energy from the onslaught of heat and humidity. The downside is the need to constantly scan the trail and the horizon for signs of landmines and snipers. I sit on the passenger side with a steely sense of alertness, hoping the sandbags will shield us from a sudden blast. Shifting the gears frequently, Clarkee is moving us first faster, then slower, and winding, turning, and bumping over the trail. An occasional remark passes between us about the terrain, the tree line, the condition of the road, the heat, or some object on the horizon.

A deadly incident is fresh in our minds. A road mine blew up a jeep like ours, loaded with advisors from another MAT team. Coincidently, the supply chopper was overhead when it happened, and Ishmael 11 was able to report the entire gruesome event over his radio as he witnessed it. We heard the whole thing on our field radio many klicks away. Captain Brown, Sergeant Johnson, and their interpreter, Trung si Ky, had been traveling the dirt road leading to the Huu Dinh Forest, a peninsula across the river from Ben Tre. The explosion upended their jeep, shattering the floorboards and scattering sandbags up into the air. Brown and Johnson were thrown out onto the road while the jeep careened into a ditch with the interpreter in the back seat bleeding from shrapnel wounds.

Ishmael 11 called in a rescue team and troops to secure the area. Captain Brown was killed instantly by the blast; Sergeant Johnson died in the medevac on the way to Saigon. The interpreter survived his wounds and eventually returned to duty. Glued to our field radio, we listened to the whole horrible series of events described by the pilot. The harshness of the incident took us all aback, while knowing full well that it could be us next time. Mourning the loss of our fellow team members, we vowed to be more vigilant in recognizing the dangers around us. Now, going down this trail, our eyes are peeled for land mines.

We arrive in An Thanh by midafternoon, tense from being on constant alert. The muscles in my shoulders relax a bit as the jeep pulls in front of the main strong point on the outer edge of the village. The main stronghold is constructed of mud and sandbag walls attached to a small pagoda. It is the headquarters of a popular force platoon under the direction of the village chief. The backside of the stronghold has deep, hard, mud trenches that give the platoon clear fields of fire behind the village out over rice paddies. The front of this stronghold looks out over the village square and is almost a hundred yards from the town landing on the river. Across the river from the town landing is a second outpost arranged in a triangle constructed of the usual mud, sandbags, and concertina wire. It has a tower on each of the three corners.

The village chief is a prosperous merchant who lives in a cement house across from the main stronghold. As we pull up he walks out of his house toward us. He is a thin middle-aged man with an air of confidence dressed in creased cotton trousers, a green patterned short sleeve, button-up shirt, and a porkpie hat. Sergeant Clarkson and I step out of the jeep to greet him.

He extends his arm for a handshake and says, "Chao Trung uy, Trung si."

He says this with the expectation we know the Vietnamese words for first lieutenant and sergeant, the usual greeting for advisors when proper names are unfamiliar.

I respond with "Chao, Truong Than," the greeting for village chief.

After shaking our hands he nods to Doc and Trung si Sang.

By this time the platoon leader has walked across the street from the stronghold to join us. He is dressed similarly to the village chief with the addition of an M1 carbine slung over his shoulder. We say our greetings and shake hands with a slight bow. Sergeant Sang interprets the rest.

We find out that the platoon sets ambushes three times a week and has had one man wounded in a skirmish with a handful of VC. The fort across the waterway from the dock takes hostile fire from small arms every few days. Other than that things are "tot," the Vietnamese word for good. The chief emphasizes that this is a "number one village," the platoon leader is "number one," and just about everything around is "number one." He even allows that we are "number one." This information gives me the feeling that the local forces have an edge on the VC but something could happen at any time, especially at night.

The platoon leader invites us to inspect the popular force soldiers' rifles and equipment, which, it turns out, are in good operating order. After that, the village chief invites us to drink tea on the patio of his house overlooking the town square. I am thinking that this little scene sends a symbolic message to the passing villagers that it is safe here and the chief is secure in his relationship with Americans. Word of this small bit of diplomacy will probably spread out into the surrounding countryside to VC who dominate hamlets and patches of jungle. Who knows what attacks it will prevent. Since we plan to stay here a few days that thought is encouraging. In any case, drinking tea in a secure place is a nice break from the delta mud.

———

The next day Doc Jackson and I are headed to the district capital of Tanh Phu Village on the water taxi. We plan to get an intelligence briefing from our district boss, Major Grady, and pick up some medical supplies. It is nice to know that Doc is a good shot. Our trip will take us up the river about three klicks. The water taxi is the easiest way since the roads are washed out, preventing the jeep from passing; and Doc figures the VC will probably not attack with twenty or so Vietnamese in the boat, we hope. So we get on the roof of the boat and lay down with our rifles at the ready. Waiting a few moments for the boat to depart I become acutely aware of the dead fish stink rising from the dock area, the place where small fishing boats tie up and offload their catch for sale at the market only a few paces away.

The trip to district goes well. People are crammed into the seats in the cabin below along with their sacks of rice, dried shrimp, and a few clucking chickens. A better price for farm produce can be had in the district town. Motoring slowly but calmly through the water, the motion of the boat gives me a sense of peace and tranquility. Blue sky covers the spread of rice paddies, separated by dark green treetops and thickets of scrub. Recalling my views from helicopters, I imagine this boat as a speck on one of many waterways flowing through the flat expanse of delta. It would be nice to enjoy the beautiful countryside without having to worry about getting lit up at any second.

On the return trip we are back on the roof of the boat. I reflect on our visit. We had updated Major Grady on our activities and then received an intelligence briefing from Captain Watson, the district intelligence officer.

He said the VC are operating in squad-sized units and regularly harassing our outposts, but he has no evidence that they are gathering forces for a major attack. But, he said that could happen at any time so make sure our Vietnamese troops don't get complacent. Other than that cheery piece of news, Doc is real happy that he was able to get a fresh load of medical supplies. I am happy because I picked up a Smith and Wesson .357 magnum revolver for a hundred bucks from one of the guys who bought it, in turn, from a pilot. Who knows where it was before that? But, it holds six rounds of .38s or .357s and it shoots well; and it is supposed to be more accurate than one of those army issue .45s.

We are going down the river. The boat passes by fishermen casting their nets in the water. Away past the river banks there are rice paddies with occasional patches of thick vegetation. In places leafy vegetation grows close to the mud banks. I look extra carefully at these spots because they can easily conceal an enemy. We round a bend in the river and I see a clump of trees about fifty meters ahead. There is a dark shadow in the trees that does not look natural. It is different from the other shadows and I think it moved. I feel my pulse quicken and my breathing gets shallow. The adrenalin quickens my senses and my eyes narrow on the spot.

"Doc," I whisper, "on the right, ahead fifty meters."

He looks at me and nods while he clicks the safety off his weapon. My weapon is ready to go, my finger poised over the trigger. The boat gets closer to the tree clump. There is movement in the trees, but I see no weapons, no muzzle flash. My finger lightly touches the trigger on my M16. Then I see that the shadow is a young boy lying on a fallen tree trunk with a fishing line in his hand.

"Hold it, Doc," I say in a clear voice.

"Jeez," he says sharply, "we almost smoked that kid."

"Lucky," I say. "Lucky for him, lucky for us!"

The boat passes the kid. He waves. We wave. Maybe he is just a kid fishing. Maybe he is a VC spy. Who knows? The tension in my limbs ebbs. I resume watching the tree line. It will be nice to get back to the village... only one more klick.

When we see the village dock I feel that we will be all right. I picture our hooch in the village fort where there is a big bucket of water for washing. We paid a mamasan to fill it with river water; a big luxury in this hot climate since there is no plumbing.

I say, "Doc, it would be nice to wash off. How about you?"

He replies, "That's nice, LT, but, you know, if Charlie don't get you that river water will."

"Wha'da you mean, Doc?"

"Well, you heard of Admiral Zumwalt, right?"

"Yes," I reply. "He's the one in charge of the navy river boats, the brown water navy, right?"

"Yep," says Doc, "but he ordered that they spray a herbicide on the jungle around the river...dioxin or Agent Orange I think it is. That's so Charlie can't fire on our river boats from cover."

"So, what's wrong with that?" I say.

"Well, you get enough of that stuff an' you're gonna die like a withered up jungle vine."

"Ah," I say, "How much of that stuff did they spray around here?"

Doc replies, "I dunno, LT, but it's all the same river water; so if they sprayed it upriver then it's down here: it's in the mud and it's gonna be in us."

"Maybe, Doc," I say, "but it looks OK here on this canal. I'm hot, just want to rinse off and we haven't died from it yet."

"Yeah" says Doc, "We don't have much choice so I'll flip you for the first wash."

"Right," I say.

———

That night, our team is staying in the sandbag and mud-walled stronghold next to the pagoda. There is a tin roof reinforced with timbers and salvaged steel fence posts piled with a few layers of sandbags to protect against enemy rockets and mortars. We can see out over the paddies beyond the village in the clear night. On the other side, the village square is quiet and empty. A few of the village soldiers stand guard, rifles slung casually over their shoulders or held in their laps as they sit. A squad of the popular forces is out on ambush along one of the major trails leading into the village.

We string our hammocks between the thick poles that hold up the roof. The poles are just right to stretch out the hammocks and let us swing a little, a small comfort in our primitive surroundings. Our rifles, extra bandoliers of M16 ammo, TA50 web belts with grenades, ammo pouches, and canteens are leaning against the dried mud walls. Doc is lying in his hammock and listening to his cassette player. Sergeant Clarkson and I are swinging and listening to one of the popular force soldiers singing outside in the night air.

I am scribbling a letter to my wife, Cathy. My words describe the beauty of Vietnam and the friendliness of the villagers. There is no mention of VC, booby traps, and wounded soldiers. I ask about our baby daughter and how my parents are doing. Then there are ideas about places for R&R, meaning a short leave for rest and relaxation.

For R&R, Cathy picked Hawaii over Japan or Hong Kong as soon as she knew it was a possibility. I guess she wants a change of climate from New England since she was born and raised outside of Boston. We met at Boston University in the hiking club. Swinging in my hammock in this hot, muggy night I recall how we hiked in the crisp autumn air of Massachusetts, seeing leaves of every color. After this brief reverie I sigh and finish the letter fully aware that I am in a very different place.

When I fold the thin paper and stuff it into the airmail envelope, Sergeant Clarkson says, "LT, this is a pretty quiet village. It looks like they have their act together. Should we worry about the guard tonight?"

"Well, that platoon leader has a reputation for being tough and dedicated; they have security out so I think we can rest easy, Clarkee."

"OK," he says.

A few moments later he says, "It is too bad about Captain Blake getting that Dear John letter."

"Yeah," I reply. "He's over here six months, getting ready for R&R and wham, she sends him a letter saying she is in love with another guy. At least they have no children."

Clarkson says, "Yeah, the other guy is not even a soldier. He is some guy with a high draft number so he can stay safe and snake some soldier's wife. It ain't right!"

"You're right, Clarkee."

We swing for a few moments on our hammocks contemplating all of this. The singing popular force soldier sends his song quietly into the night. The hissing kerosene lamp spreads a yellow glow into the shadows of the hooch.

Sergeant Clarkson looks over and says, "The Captain took it hard at first, with cussing, and ranting about the lousy, sneaky lover boys back in the states who take advantage of GIs. Then he said maybe she didn't love him after all; maybe she got distracted with him being away; maybe she gave him up for a dead man when he left for the Nam."

"Is there any fairness in love and war?" I ask.

"I don't know, but I am over here on my second tour and my wife hasn't left me yet. I hope I make it back, then three more years and we retire to farming in Arkansas."

"Nice plan," I say. "I hope it all works out."

After a few moments of silence, we hear automatic rifle fire in the distance.

"Sounds like M16s and AK-47s," says Clarkson.

We listen, for a few seconds, instinctively trying to gauge how far away and in what direction the firing is coming from. Sergeant Clarkson looks at me and says, "It's in the back, about two clicks."

We jump out of our hammocks and rush to the back wall to look out over the paddies. Sure enough, we see muzzle flashes from the last outpost we had inspected on the way to An Thanh. The little fort is taking fire from the jungle behind it, maybe from a squad of VC. An RPG flashes from the bush and hits the side of the fort. There are spurts of fire alternating between the sharp cracking of M16s and the deeper popping from AK-47s. The night duel continues as if the VC are determined to wear the defenders down. Sooner or later someone will run out of ammunition and the fort does not have a big supply.

Sergeant Clarkson says, "LT, how about a fire mission?"

I turn and nod, saying, "Let's do it. Charles is about one hundred meters behind the fort."

He gets on the field radio and reaches district head-quarters where there is a battery of 105s. Holding the handset close to his cheek, he says, "Foxtrot One Six, this is Roughneck Three Two."

"Roughneck Three Two, this is Foxtrot One Six."

"This is Roughneck Three Two, fire mission, enemy squad in the trees, grid coordinates 653172, direction 185 mils, distance two zero, zero, zero meters. Fire one HE, danger close friendlies. I will adjust."

"This is Foxtrot One Six, roger copy 653172, direction 185, distance two thousand, fire one HE marking round, danger close, over."

We wait a long half-minute and hear: "This is "Foxtrot One Six, shot over."

The round hits right on target.

"Foxtrot One Six, this is Roughneck Three Two, shot on target, fire six rounds for effect, over."

"This is Foxtrot One Six, copy six rounds for effect"

Five seconds later the handset barks, "Shots over!"

We wait a few seconds and hear the *whump, wawhump, wawhumphump* of rounds hitting the ground. Then there is silence.

Clarkson says, "I think Charles stopped firing just after the marking round; probably moved out of the area."

I say, "Yep, Mr. Charles is doing just what Uncle Ho wants him to do, hit and run, wear us out; live to fight another day."

He picks up the handset and says, "Foxtrot One Six, this is Roughneck Three Two, unknown casualties. End fire mission, over."

The response comes back from Foxtrot. "Copy unknown casualties, end fire mission."

"This Roughneck Three Two, thanks for the help, out."

———

The next morning, before full daylight, we hear a commotion outside. Sergeant Sang is already talking in Vietnamese to the platoon leader. Outside, I see a squad of bedraggled and worried men. They are the night ambush squad with three of the seven men wounded. They had a bad tangle with more VC than they wanted. They had the drop on the VC but their intended victims fought back fiercely with grenades and small arms. Our squad fell back with two men getting arm and leg wounds and a third cracking his skull on a fence post or rock.

Picking up his medical bag, Doc says firmly, "bring 'em into the pagoda so I can work on 'em."

He and Sang put thick field dressings on the two with bullet wounds on their limbs. He tells me to hold a lantern over the head of the guy with the cracked skull. I nod at Sergeant Clarkson when he points to the radio, knowing that he wants to call for help.

Doc says, "He won't die right now."

As I hold the lantern over the wounded man, I hear Clarkson on the radio calling in a medevac and start to pick up his radio call:

"This is Roughneck Three Two. Coordinates are same as our night location, three friendlies need medevac, status is priority."

"This is Foxtrot Six Five, chopper will be on site in three zero mikes. Standby to pop smoke."

I am holding the lantern over the man who is bleeding from a long gash on his skull. The skin is cut open and I can see the bone. The squeamish feeling in my gut confirms my inadequacy in dealing with this emergency medical stuff. I am thinking that this guy might

die right here. Doc gets out a needle and thread and
starts stitching the skin back into place. He pushes the
needle through the swollen, split skin and pulls the
thread across the split. With each stitch he pulls the
skin together and amazingly the wound closes up so
the blood only weeps through. Each time he pushes the
needle through the soldier gasps and tightens up, even
though he is still dazed from his fall. I clench my teeth
with each stroke of the needle and try to concentrate on
holding the lantern over the bleeding skull without getting sick to my stomach.

Finally, Doc says, "That ought to hold him until he
gets to the hospital."

I take a deep breath and say, "Doc, you're amazing!
Thanks."

He looks at me as if it were just a cake walk and
responds, "Nothing to it LT, its all in a day's work here
in the Nam."

The radio is active again: "Roughneck Three Two,
this is Medevac Four Niner, ETA your position in one
mike. Any enemy contact your location? Stand by to pop
smoke."

"This is Roughneck Three Two. Roger Medevac Four
Niner. No enemy contact on our Lima Zulu. Smoke is
out."

Sergeant Clarkson is on the landing zone. He pops a smoke grenade that billows out yellow smoke. The radio unit is in one hand and the handset is in the other.

"Roughneck three two, this is Medevac Four Niner I copy yellow smoke."

"Medevac Four Niner, this is Roughneck Three Two, that is affirmative on yellow smoke."

We hear the thumping of the chopper rotors as the Huey comes in low over the tree line. We carry the wounded to the landing zone as the bird hovers for a moment over the clearing and then sets down, rotors still spinning. After loading our wounded we give a thumbs up to the crew chief at the side door. The chopper rises as we run away to the front, staying clear of the dangerous tail rotor, so we can avoid having our heads taken off.

The sun is rising higher on another day in the Republic of Vietnam. Warm, humid air has already pushed away the night chill. The village market comes to life as farmers bring in their produce. Children play in the streets. Fishermen cast their nets on the river. The scene is a picture of peacefulness...peacefulness amid chaos. The village is one domino among all of the villages and hamlets of this country. In turn, this country is one domino in the minds of policy makers in Washington D.C. I think, maybe peace will come to this village someday.

Seven

CU CHI

Only two days after meeting Thinh and Than, his new friends from the north, Hiep is gathering supplies back in his hamlet. He gets word from runners, boys from other hamlets, that an American force is in the area and moving toward the tunnels of Cu Chi. Hiep is not too surprised at this. Cu Chi is the center of a continued, strong resistance and has been ever since the French tried to dominate the land. It is only twenty-five miles northwest of Saigon, the seat of the puppet government. Hiep knows Cu Chi is an embarrassment to the Americans and to President Thieu. They must strike often and hope to wipe it out.

Back in the tunnels that night, Hiep warns his friends of the impending sweep of Cu Chi by the Americans.

"Do not worry friends," says Hiep. "Our tunnels have given us the advantage for a long time and they will give us protection now. We will kill some GIs and escape. Look at these M16 rifles we captured from dead Americans. Now we will use their own weapons against them."

Thinh says, "We are with you, brother. Show us how you fight in the South."

Duong Tan Phong is responsible for the overall resistance efforts of several hamlets in this sector. He listens to this talk, but now he speaks up and says, "We have a plan for this type of situation. We will shoot and move near the outer hamlets and then pull back to the tunnels while we confuse the Americans and inflict casualties. We have already set up operations in three hamlets."

Looking at Thinh and Thanh he says, "I ask you to go to the Xom Moi Hamlet to join the fighting there. Hiep has led the fighters there before and the people hate the Americans. Hit the enemy and then pull back to the tunnels. I will coordinate the efforts of the three fighting groups with runners. Meet back here if all goes well."

Hiep, Thinh, and Thanh arrive near Xom Moi just after four in the morning. The trio huddles with a dozen other fighters in a dugout as the Americans start shelling the area. Hiep surveys the weapons these fighter carry. He has made it a point to learn about the variety of weapons available, part of the expertise that has earned him a leadership position. Eight of the hamlet fighters are armed with AK-47s or M16s. Two carry the captured French MAS 49-56 semiautomatic rifle with a ten-round magazine and 7.5 x 54mm ammo. Two others carry the French MAS 36 bolt-action rifle with a five-round magazine, also with the 7.5 x 54mm ammo. He and his two friends from the north carry AK-47s. Hiep recalls his admiration for the MAS 49-56, a fine battle rifle. It is simple like the AK-47, accurate like the M16, and fires a powerful round like the American M14s. But the ammo is not easily available so it is best used in areas like this near a supply center. After these thoughts run through his mind, he notices a slowdown in the shelling.

Hiep turns to Thinh and says, "The government and their allies shell our villages without regard for women, children, and old people. This shows how little they care about the poor people of this country."

"It is like this all over," replies Thinh

"The worse the government treats them, the more people will like us," adds Thanh.

With the first pale light of morning the shelling stops. The VC move to a good vantage point under trees overlooking a clear area.

Hiep says, "The Americans have artillery and gunships so it is not a good idea to engage them at this distance. It is better to let them approach until they are almost on top of us. We want to close in with our enemies so we are almost hanging onto their belts. That way they have less advantage over us with their long range weapons."

The first american comes within fifty yards of them. The gunships have moved off to cover another hamlet, possibly, Hiep thinks, because Phong is stirring things up over there. To his front only five of the advancing Americans, well spread out, can be seen in the clearing.

Looking over at Thinh, Hiep says, "I've been in situations like this many times before. The Americans will behave predictably. They are not mad yet so when we shoot they will take cover and call in shells and gunships to hit our tree line. After the heat of fighting, they might be more aggressive."

"We will follow your lead," replies Thinh with a nod.

In a hushed voice Thanh says, "I wonder how many are behind the advance element?"

"We will find out when we hit and run," replies Hiep in a whisper.

Hiep signals with his hands for the fighters to fire fast but cut if off quickly and move out.

The VC fighters fire several bursts of automatic fire at the Americans. It seems to take longer but lasts only a few seconds. Two of the Americans are hit immediately. The others take cover behind tree stumps or in ditches. The wounded call out for medics. Hiep's fighters move to another vantage point away from the expected onslaught of shells on their first position.

Well camouflaged, the VC fighters wait more than an hour for the Americans to move toward them again. They are now positioned under a tree line near one of the outer tunnels of Cu Chi. The fighters have deployed themselves in a V formation instead of a straight line to catch the enemy in a cross fire. Hiep can see the Americans advancing. Once again the gunships have moved away to another location.

Thanh looks up at the sky and asks, "Why have the gunships left?"

Hiep smiles with tight lips and says, "They may have been called away. Or, if the Americans have a large force they may be confidant that we are too few to fight them. Maybe they think we have run off."

Thanh nods and says, "That should give us the advantage of surprise."

"Yes," says Hiep, and the tunnels give us an edge too."

Hiep pauses, and says, "I grew up here and now we will show them how we treat unwanted visitors."

As the American troops move closer, Hiep signals again for rapid fire, but then to hold the position.

The VC open up, firing a torrent of bullets at the Americans. Two more GIs go down. For a moment, Hiep's fighters hold their fire as if they had again retreated. More Americans move forward. They spread out and then form a protective perimeter around their wounded men and also start trying to maneuver against the VC. The VC fighters pour on an intense, withering fire. Bullets are flying everywhere in the clearing, but the GIs have good cover on the ground. Only two more are hit. The GIs seem confused about the direction of the attack but they fire into the jungle tree line. None of the VC fighters are hit. Hiep signals that it is time to move to the nearest tunnel.

All of the VC fighters find their way to a cave-like room three levels down in the tunnels. The room has escape tunnels in three directions in case one of them collapses. There is only enough room to crouch or sit up. The American artillery fire is hitting the ground around them.

Between the earth-dulled blasts Hiep says, "We have done well so far. At least six Americans down, but it will be a long day. Reload your weapons and rest. Then we will go out again."

The fighters nod and grin with quiet murmurs of assent and nervous chuckling.

On the next venture out, after the shelling stops, Hiep and his fighters move to a new location. Shortly, an American squad, nine or ten men, comes into view. They are trying to flank Hiep's previous location.

Turning to Thanh, Hiep says, "They are still trying to penetrate this area. Their persistence deserves some respect."

"When you respect your adversaries, there is more honor when they are vanquished," replies Thanh.

Thinh and Hiep nod their heads in agreement and then look out toward the open area where they see a second group of enemy, a platoon of twenty-five or thirty men.

Thinh says, "They know we are giving them a fight so they brought more men."

In this new position, the VC can fire into the Americans with a killing effect. They pour fire into the GIs who immediately drop to the ground. The GIs are disciplined and have maintained a good distance between themselves. This helps them to survive. Two or three GIs are wounded in the initial burst of fire, but the others find cover behind stumps, logs, and mounds of earth. Some of the GIs return fire. M16 rounds hit the branches around the VC. An M79 grenade launched by a GI falls short of its mark but sprays dirt and debris over the VC. The bullets spit into the ground around them and splinter tree branches. There is a lull after the first fierce moments of fighting and targets are harder to find. Hiep calculates whether it is worth continuing the fight.

The seconds tick on. Then some Americans begin to maneuver while others direct an intense hail of bullets at the VC. With the larger force and more firepower the Americans can force their way toward Hiep and his fighters. The VC return fire and then start an orderly retreat. Half the fighters fire at the GIs while the others run rearward; they switch roles in a well-practiced fire and maneuver retreat away from the GIs. But the American attack is intense. The VC are hard-pressed. One of the local fighters is hit in the leg while running. Thinh sees the wounded man and stops to help him get up. Thinh and the wounded fighter limp toward the rear. Then Thinh is struck in the arm by a bullet. Others come to help the two wounded men.

The VC rear guard increases the rate of fire. They shoot on full automatic, blasting off their rounds at a fierce rate. Rifle barrels get hot to the touch from the stream of bullets. They are determined to stop the

American attack. The Americans once again slow down to tend to their wounded and regroup. The VC fighters take advantage of the opportunity to escape to the protection of a tunnel. Hiep directs the fighters to take the wounded first and to make sure there are no blood trails leading to the tunnel.

Thanh bends over Thinh and says, "You're very brave my brother. You have helped this wounded man to escape."

Thinh grimaces from the pain in his arm and grunts acknowledgement. The two wounded are treated with medical supplies in the tunnel, but Thinh's arm is broken and will need more attention. The other man has only a flesh wound in the leg. Hiep thinks, these wounds will heal, so we are lucky.

Helicopters can be heard overhead flying back and forth, searching for some sign of the VC. Occasionally the helicopters shoot rockets at some presumed target. Hiep thinks, our tunnels have such small openings that it would be very difficult for a rocket or bomb to get in. He feels a little less tense. The words of Uncle Ho come back to him: "A stork can't shit in a bottle, so with our tunnels we shouldn't be scared of American bombers." Hiep imagines a giant stork with the body of a large airplane flying overhead showering bombs down on everything except the tunnel opening. He smiles and relaxes some more. He wants to repeat Ho Chi Minh's words of wisdom but thinks it is better to keep quiet in the tunnel in case there are American troops who might hear them laughing.

It is not long before the VC hear American voices outside the tunnel opening. The opening is about five meters away around a bend and up one level but the voices travel down to them. Hiep does not need to signal for the VC fighters to be quiet and still. Everyone is frozen and looking intently toward the tunnel entrance. Hiep is thinking, what would Uncle Ho say about this situation? Maybe a stork can't shit in a bottle, but a snake can crawl down a hole. He knows what is coming.

It is quiet for a few long moments and then Hiep signals for the fighters to cover their ears. All the fighters quickly hold their hands over their ears and put their faith and hope in the ability of the earth to hold back an explosion.

Loud voices penetrate the earth above. Then there is silence. A grenade explodes in the tunnel. Hiep thinks, the GIs are predictable. They want to go down the tunnel but they prefer to toss a grenade in first. Would one of them be brave enough to enter and wiggle through the maze? No, they are too large for that.

In a few minutes they hear an American cursing, his voice muffled by the walls of the tunnel. They hear the scrape of his boots pushing on dirt. Then they hear the voice say, "Lieutenant, I'm stuck. This lousy gook hole is too small for me. Help me out." There is a lot of noise, scuffling, and cursing but eventually the voice says, "I'm glad to get out of that hell hole. Couldn't get very far but didn't see any gooks either. Maybe they got scared away. Can't we just blow it?"

Hiep whispers sharply to the others, "Watch out! This time they will use a bigger explosive. But, if the hole caves in they will think it is a victory and go away."

They wait for a very long moment, barely breathing, hands over their ears. There is a big explosion. Only a little dust and dirt comes into their tunnel-room after the concussion. The walls of the tunnel have absorbed most of the blast.

Thanh speaks to no one in particular, "My ears are ringing but I can still hear."

Hiep looks at Thanh and says, "We are lucky. We hit eight or nine of the enemy and they wasted a lot of men, time, and ammunition for very little gain. We should rest."

Thanh replies, "This is good practice for our mission in Ben Tre. Too bad we will have to leave Thinh here for his arm to heal; but he can fight with these good people and help them learn the wisdom of Uncle Ho."

Eight

TEAM REUNION

We are back at Firebase Bravo after a week in Ap An Thanh. The guys are sitting around in our plywood and sandbag hooch, updating our team logbook, finishing reports, cleaning weapons, and drinking Sergeant Bradford's freshly brewed coffee. We review our visits to An Thanh, An Quy, and other popular force locations assigned to us in the Tan Phu District. Talk turns to the beauty of the countryside and the peaceful views of farmers knee deep in rice paddies, boys herding the family water buffalo, and fishermen gracefully casting their nets in waterways. Contrasted to these pleasant recollections are the fears of explosives on the roads and trails, snipers in the tree line, and the difficulty of walking through boot-sucking mud in the canals.

Captain Blake is holding a plastic coffee cup in his left hand while he inspects a fine looking .45-caliber pistol in his right. He seems to have recovered from the "Dear John" letter from his wife. At first he had angrily questioned how it could happen. He was filled with frustration in being too far away to do much about it. He started writing a letter asking her to change her mind, but then ripped it up in a fit of rage saying, "It's too late. It has gone too far. It's over!" He succumbed to the fact that she took comfort in the arms of another man who was there with her, not off on the other side of the world. Maybe she doesn't love him; maybe she fell out of love with him because he is willing to fight in this controversial war; maybe she needs constant attention; maybe she can't stand the feeling that her love is wasted on a soldier who could come home to her cold and lifeless.

Captain Blake had been feeling down and depressed about his ruined marriage, but at last he did get a boost. It was a package from his father that had arrived on the supply chopper. He and his father had shared a love of the sport of competitive pistol shooting. The package contained a pair of match grade .45 caliber pistols each in a black leather holster. The pistols are similar to the standard issue army pistols but more finely produced for a high level of accuracy in competitive matches. They were almost objects of art with engraved scrolls on the barrels and rosewood grips highly polished to show the beautiful grain of the wood.

A note from Captain Blake's father had accompanied the pistols. It expressed how much the senior Blake had enjoyed their teamwork and the pride he feels for his son's service to his country. It also expressed the wish that the match set of pistols would give his son a special advantage over the enemy and help bring his son home safely.

Using the Vietnamese word for captain, Sergeant Clarkson puts down his coffee cup and says, "Dai uy, those are sure some beautiful looking hog legs you have there."

"Thank you Clarkee, they sure are," replies Blake as he looks admiringly at the pistol held up in his right hand. "These babies are Colt .45 Gold Cups with specially calibrated barrels, upgraded triggers and hammers, and inner parts that are polished for smooth operation. Plus, look at these double diamond rosewood grips."

As we are trying to take all that in, he looks at us and says, "Hey, do you want to see how they work?"

"Yes," we say almost in unison.

We go outside to a pile of sandbags set up for target practice at the edge of the compound. The regional force company commander likes to see his soldiers practice marksmanship on a regular basis. Blake locks and loads a seven-round magazine of .45 caliber ammunition in each of his beauties.

Then he holsters them and says, "See those tin cans in front of the sandbags?"

He gestures to nine fifteen-ounce cans resting on a log about fifty feet away.

We all nod our heads as Sergeant Clarkson says, "Yuh, they would equal the size of Charlie's head at two hundred feet."

We all looked again, as if to verify this pronouncement, realizing that Clarkee is a light weapons expert.

After seeing everyone nod again, Captain Blake draws his right-side weapon with a smooth motion and holds it in a two-armed shooter's stance. He proceeds to fire in a smooth, steady rhythm with the *Blam, Blam, Blam* of the .45 echoing around the walls of the firebase. Each time he fires a can jumps off the log. He follows up with a second shot on one can, making it bounce again. In a matter of a few seconds of steady semiautomatic fire he upsets a half dozen cans without missing a shot. Then he holsters the pistol and draws the left side weapon while at the same time going down on one knee as if taking cover behind a tree. He holds this pistol in his right hand and fires again at the cans. The remaining three cans fly off the log and each is hit again with a follow-up shot. Only one shot misses.

We all stand back in awe of this demonstration. Some of the Vietnamese soldiers have gathered around and are talking excitedly while pointing at the cans. A few of them say, "Dai uy number one." They hold up their first finger and say "number one." We all admire the skill displayed in this demonstration. In less than one-half minute Blake could have dispatched over a dozen enemies. No one speculates what his accuracy would be if the enemy were running and trying to hide, because none of us can shoot a .45 like that. Of course the ones the army issues aren't as well made.

"Mighty fine shooting Dai uy," says Sergeant Clarkson.

"That would give Charlie a headache all day long," adds Sergeant Bradford.

I say, "Mighty impressive boss. I'm glad you're on our side."

Back in the hooch, Captain Blake expresses new joy over the pistols. He is visibly buoyed up by the success of his demonstration and our admiring comments. He loves the precision and beauty of the pistols and the connection with his father. To him, the protective aura of his father is around the pistols. He expresses his confidence that with the pistols he could deal with anything and overcome all odds. They seem to take away the pain his wife has inflicted upon him. It seems to me that they help to encourage his inner strength and to find a vision of gallantry and glory that overcomes his wife's words of broken love.

———

Later on, we are sorting through a bag of mail and supplies dropped off by chopper.

Captain Blake looks up from an official order and says, "Well, gentlemen, we are going to be making the change we've been waiting for. This is a confirmation that we're going to move north of Ben Tre next week. You know that Charlie has been making the colonel nuts. There he is with his province headquarters in Ben Tre where he is supposed to be an example of pacification, but Victor Charles keeps dropping rockets right around the colonel's compound. They want us to go on a special mission with a lien doi battalion to intercept VC and keep them from attacking Ben Tre."

"What's a lien doi battalion?" I ask.

Blake nods. "The basic term means a battalion made of three infantry companies. But I get the impression that these are hand picked units with good fighting reputations. Plus, our guys are reinforced with a heavy weapons platoon, so we will have mortars and more machine guns."

We all nod affirmatively as we take in this information.

I remember the rocket that fell just short of the old French hotel during my first days in the province, and the eight dead Navy Seals when I first arrived in Ben Tre. I picture the old French administration buildings on the main street of Ben Tre with bullet marks on the walls. No doubt the colonel thinks the VC are all around and will continue to take every opportunity to undermine our efforts.

Blake says, "Victor Charles even dropped a few rockets right on the old man's chopper pad. That would definitely interrupt the mail run and beer supply for the senior officers."

We all laugh at that one, especially since we get too few opportunities to get away from our base and into the relative luxury of the Ben Tre compound where there are mess hall meals and hot showers.

Clarkee adds, "They can't have VC rockets interrupt chow time in the mess hall."

We all nod our heads and smile while we look at Blake to continue his briefing.

Blake is sketching a map of the Ben Tre area, with an arrow showing how the VC fire rockets across a river a few klicks north of the city. The province advisor's compound and the Vietnamese headquarters are well within easy range of the rockets. We all gather around the table as he points to the sketch.

Tapping a finger on the western edge of the map, he looks up and continues, "The lien doi battalion has already started search and clear operations on the western edge of the Huu Dinh Peninsula, with only moderate resistance from Mr. Charles. The mission is to kick the VC off the peninsula and set up a string of forts to keep them from crossing over from one side of the peninsula to the other with their rockets."

Clarkee says, "Yeah, the VC bring rockets by water on the north side of the peninsula. That river is not too secure so it's easy access for them, hard to intercept 'em."

"Right," adds Blake. "Now we are going to get in there with a crack lien doi outfit and kick some butt."

He pencils in the location of three abandoned mud forts and also draws the one dirt road from the district town into the heart of the Huu Dinh. He says, "This will be our general approach."

"Only one problem," says Sergeant Bradford. "The road from the district into the Huu Dinh is where Captain Brown and Sergeant Johnson got blown away by a road mine. Remember, we heard the whole thing on the radio."

"Yeah," says Blake. "That's why we're going by chopper. They are going to insert us in a jungle clearing near our battalion."

"Now we're talking," I say. "I'll carry the M60."

"Yeah," says Bradford. "Charlie may be waiting for us. We better hit the ground and be ready to lay down some heat."

I picture our team spreading out from the chopper and hitting the ground with weapons at the ready, looking for enemy muzzle flashes from the surrounding jungle. There will be six of us, including Trung si Sang. We will bring the M60 machine gun and the M79 grenade launcher and maybe a few M72 LAW antitank weapons plus our M16s. The M60 will put out heavy bursts and tamp down an enemy attack. Then I realize that with the M60 in my hands Charlie will focus on me as a prime target. I hope we will take them by surprise before they can organize a reception.

We all start talking about how we need to prepare for our combat insertion. The call for action has us all charged up. We are also excited by the change from village-hamlet security and routine patrols to more aggressive combat operations, moving from mostly defensive to offensive.

After some discussion we plan to operate in two teams with alternating assignments. One team will operate with the battalion headquarters element and the reserve infantry company. The other team will go with one of the other two infantry companies. We will also alternate going into the district or province every few days to rest, resupply and coordinate plans with the higher command. Initially, one team will be Captain Blake and Clarkee along with a popular force interpreter. The other team will be me and Brad along with Trung si Sang, our team interpreter. Doc will rotate between the teams as needed.

After days of packing and planning we are nearly ready to move. A big Chinook helicopter will pick us up later in the day with our equipment, jeep, and everything but the plywood hooch. The local infantry company commander is eager to take over our hooch and possibly invite the artillery lieutenant to share it. He will be happy to switch from his sandbag bunker to the relative comfort of a plywood floor and tin roof. Yesterday he came over with a bottle of bac si de, or home made rice whisky. We all drank a toast to our alliance and to the future. The bac si de reminded me of lighter fluid. It left my throat raw and produced instant heartburn. It was almost as if I had swallowed kerosene. Most of us declined another round, but Captain Blake had one more to show his solidarity with the commander.

———

Brad and I are cleaning the M60 machine gun. We are breaking it down into the eight parts groups usually maintained by a gunner. The hooch is filled with the smells of spent gunpowder and the petroleum sweet smell of oil on metal just cleaned with solvent. The rest of the team is outside making the rounds of the compound.

Brad says, "These lien doi are strac...good reputation. Been at this a long time. Dedicated to defending their homeland. Too many other Vietnamese troops are draftees or sketchy local militia."

"Yeah, a hard-core unit sounds good," I say.

Brad continues, "The good soldiers might come from a long line of fighters. War in this country goes back at least two thousand years, when the Chinese invaded."

"Yeah," I say. "That's a big legacy."

Brad nods and says, "You know, the French captured Saigon in 1861. Vietnamese fought with the French...or against them. That's a lot of time to learn the art of war."

"True, Brad, that's why Charlie knows how to fight. Maybe that's why we haven't won this war yet. It's too long."

Brad replies, "Yeah, our supposedly weaker enemy ain't so weak after all."

After detaching the barrel assembly from the M60, I run the cleaning rod through the barrel several times and say, "Brad, seems to me that you're up on your history. Did you study that in school?

"Well...I have a degree in philosophy but studied a lot of history and the other liberal arts stuff."

"Ever want OCS (Officers Candidate School)?" I ask.

"I had the opportunity but turned it down. The army paid for college, and I'm grateful for that. I just wanted to figure out what makes this crazy world tick and maybe get a handle on whether this war makes sense."

He wipes a light coating of gun oil on a few machine gun parts with a stained, white rag.

Then he says, "Also, being a second lieutenant is not the best thing right now. A lot of draftees don't like the war and don't respect the officers or the NCOs; plus we have drugs and fraggings. At least when they see my stripes they figure I might have enough experience in this green machine to help them get home."

"Hey Brad," I say. "Talking about your stripes, you're my ticket home too."

"Well LT, we'll just have to watch out for each other. How come you signed up to be an officer?"

"Oh, it seemed kind of natural...Eagle Scout, enjoy the outdoors, dad was a navy officer in World War Two, family history of service. I just believe that every citizen owes service to our country. So college ROTC seemed like a good way to go."

"Yeah, that's smart. It gives you a jump-start on the system. I have to say, though, I get satisfaction earning my stripes one by one. Plus, I have some doubts about our leadership. If I were an officer I would be one step closer to the establishment, those smart guys in Washington, D.C, who are supposed to be running this thing. It's a mess."

"Yeah Brad, but the troops still see a senior NCO as part of the system."

"Suppose so," he says.

I run a dry patch down the barrel to wipe out the solvent and carbon. "Brad, I think this war has a problem dealing with culture and politics as much as the military situation.

He says, "Yeah, I think we didn't know enough before we started."

Sliding the cleaning rod in the barrel, I say, "Now people are seeing the mess. We have these drawn out peace talks in Paris. War protestors are rioting in the streets. In 69 we had the My Lai Massacre. The Ohio National Guard killed students at Kent State. There are more and more questions about the war. Politicians don't agree on it. Things don't add up."

I pull the cleaning rod out of the barrel, replace the dirty patch, run the rod down the barrel again, and say, "We're supposed to be here to stop the spread of communism, you know, the domino theory. After all, we grew up learning to hide under our desks and go to bomb shelters because the Soviets might nuke us. So our minds are bent toward fear. But, maybe the powers that be should have done something different than this war."

Brad reflects for a moment and replies, "You know, LT, we got here bit by bit. The wheel of history turns with politics, philosophy, religion, culture, debate, good and bad thinking, and all kinds of emotions."

"So we kinda got stuck in the mud before we knew it?" I ask while running a lightly oiled patch down the barrel.

"Yeah, and it's not easy to see the way out. How do we leave without dishonoring ourselves?

I say, "Yeah, we could've done better. I think we should avoid war, except for self-defense."

Brad finishes cleaning the operating rod and bolt assemblies and looks up, "LT," he says, "do you really think humankind can avoid war?"

I pause with the cleaning rod in my hand and reply. "Sure. To me it comes down to human nature. We have the capacity for good or bad. It is just very futile when the big shots mess up."

"Right," he says.

We work on the gun in a short stretch of silence, and then I say, "Brad, you don't seem so confident in humanity. Since you're a philosopher you might have a better way to look at it."

"Well," says Brad, "history and philosophy say the behavior of mankind is pretty questionable. I mean, history is full of war for reasons that don't seem very good, and philosophers can't all agree on war."

He pauses to chuckle under his breath, "About the only thing you can hang your hat on is what Hegel said: "We learn from history that we don't learn from history.""

I respond with a laugh. "That's encouraging."

He continues. "Some philosophers say we can stop war. Others say we can't because it comes from our makeup, culture, hormones, environment, habits, or whatever. Even Socrates was a soldier."

"Yeah, Brad. We have to get beyond philosophy."

"Right." he says. "I'm just looking for clues about why my butt is in the line of fire."

"Brad, I don't know what good all the philosophers do. They spend their lives trying to split the atoms of thought, but politicians and power brokers ignore them...All the same, dumb stuff happens again. Principles are laid to waste by power, greed, ego, and fame. Even smart people succumb to their own vanity and the folly of thinking they are infallible."

He looks up from wiping the ammunition feed cover with a clean rag, "Sounds pretty negative, LT."

"No, its just cogitosis," I say with a grin.

"Cogitosis?"

"That's my word. You know, like halitosis, but sour thinking. Really, I have hope for humanity, a utilitarian view. Right action leads to happiness and wrong action leads to unhappiness, so long as one person's interests are not more important than another's. We can choose to do the right thing. Too bad if we are in the Nam for the wrong reasons. Then our actions are futile."

Brad snaps the ammunition feed cover down and says, "Uh huh...I have to think about that one."

In a playful tone I say, "OK, Brad, you're a fairly old man compared to me so you might know your own mind better than I do."

He looks at me with a puzzled expression on his face and says, "Yeah, I have been around a bit. What are you getting at?"

"Well," I say, "how long have you known yourself?"

He gives me a slightly surprised look and says, "I could say I have know myself all my life, but I suppose that's not what you mean, right?"

"Right," I say. "I mean how long have you been aware of the way you think, what you believe, how you act, what you can do, what you value, and so on."

"Well," he replies, "that's a tricky question. It's hard to know your own self. After experiencing something of the world, I am still working on it. Maybe I'll know better before I die."

"Yeah, it would be nice if we could know ourselves before getting caught up in crazy things like this war," I say.

Brad nods his head slowly, purses his slips slightly, a knowing look in his eyes.

"How did you wind up here in the Nam, Brad?"

Brad's eyes turn downward for a moment. He says, "Well, like most young men of seventeen, I got lured into the army with the usual enticements, you know, be a man, serve your country, have a career, see the world, maybe get to college, impress the girls, and that kind of stuff. Plus, my family is pretty patriotic. But now that I'm a soldier with time in the system, even if I have some doubts about this war I figure I made a bargain to serve and the most honorable thing is to do my duty. A man has to do what a man has to do. That's honorable."

I look at him respectfully and nod my head slowly before saying, "Yeah, I can understand that. I guess a lot of us are like that in one way or another. It's hard to tell what's right to do in the big scheme of things. Maybe some day it will be easier to understand it, but right now we soldier on, stand up for our country. If our country is wrong about it, we better hope there is something positive that can come out of it. Maybe we can learn from it."

Brad looks at me with a slight grimace. "Let's finish cleaning this M60," he says.

He puts the barrel back in the M60, pushes down the barrel locking lever and says, "LT, I can see what you're sayin', but right now all this stuff we are talking about, like the man says, it don't mean nothing. It don't mean nothin' because, for us, it's not complicated. We're going to the Huu Dinh Forest to give Charlie a bad time and Charlie won't like that. Its gonna be down and dirty. It's Charlie or us."

"Yeah, it's pretty simple when you put it that way," I respond.

Brad goes on, "We dodge the bullets, the punji pits, and the rockets to live another day. Then we do it all over again the next day. Maybe we win, maybe we lose, but after 365 days we're outta here. Then we take the big freedom bird home. None of that philosophy and history helps us right now. Even if the fancy pants, smart, boys in D.C. messed it up, we are still the ones out here in the boonies dealing with the nasty stuff."

I say, "You're right, Brad. I'm as happy as a toad in a boa."

He says, "Yeah, I know. I'm as happy as a toad in a boa and a duck that got run over by a truck. But the truck went off the road and hit the boa with the toad. So, which is the most out of luck, the duck or the toad?"

I reply, "Probably the driver of the truck got the worst deal, since he had to fill out the paperwork."

Brad says, "It always gets back to the paperwork."

Nine

HUU DINH VIET CONG

Dang Vu Hiep and Nguyen Tat Thanh lay in a thicket along with three local VC, behind enemy lines, at the upper end of the Huu Dinh Peninsula. They watch the activity of the ARVN soldiers who are in a French-type, triangular mud fortification with watchtowers in the three angles. Over three hundred government soldiers swept in from the West about three days ago. Those soldiers are now occupying the fort and forward areas. Hiep thinks they are from another part of Vietnam, perhaps one of President Thieu's mobile forces based near Saigon.

In a hushed voice Thanh says, "They must be disciplined because they executed their platoon movements very well."

Hiep quietly grunts assent and says, "They quickly overcame our resistance, even though we did not choose to fight them in force. Dozens of our fighters can't match the relentless tactics and firepower of these troops."

Both Hiep and Thanh know that their fighters had done well setting off land mines or popping up and firing from camouflaged spider holes in the ground. They had even killed or wounded a half dozen or so of the government soldiers. Only two VC fighters were wounded lightly and evacuated by sampan to an underground hospital to the north.

Being careful to make no sudden movements, Hiep shifts his weight slightly. He reflects on the bravery of the local fighters. They are very willing to go up against the government troops. If only more of them had automatic weapons. True, half of them are armed with Chinese Communist, or Chicom, AK-47s or the Russian SKS semiautomatic carbine with a ten-round magazine, the forerunner of the AK-47 assault rifle. But, many still carry the Chicom Type 53 bolt-action carbine with a small magazine.

Hiep muses that someone up the supply trail is doing a good job of distributing weapons and ammunition. *We have weapons that can share ammunition, and the same thing is true in Cu Chi with the captured French weapons,* he thinks. The 7.62 x 39 mm ammo is interchangeable between the AK-47 and the SKS, a good thing when supply is difficult. The Chicom Type 53 carbine is less sophisticated but it is a rugged weapon with a heavier

7.62 x 54 mm round that has good knockdown power. It is useful for long-range targets across an open field or a stream. And, Hiep thinks, the slower bolt action will tend to conserve ammunition among the less experienced fighters.

As he lay under the bushes Thanh reflects on how well he and Hiep have done in the Huu Dinh. They had arrived only a few weeks ago, having journeyed together from Cu Chi. He knows that Hiep is happy to be here, but Thanh feels especially pleased after his long journey down the Ho Chi Minh Trail from his home far in the North. He believes he has arrived in a place that is important to his destiny as a trusted representative of the powers in Hanoi. He eagerly embraces his mission to inspire the local VC fighters and to persuade the local population to support the National Liberation Front. He and Hiep are becoming knowledgeable about the local people and he is confident that he can find the words to persuade them. He also thinks his new friend Hiep, who is a capable fighter and a good combat leader, will help him be successful.

The five VC had lain in the thicket since just before dawn. The damp cool of the morning is giving way to the rising heat of day. Sunlight is streaming through the jungle canopy, warming the earth and vegetation beneath. Just as they are feeling the restless need to move away, the sound of a distant but approaching helicopter enters their awareness. Thanh moves his hand ever so slightly to signal that they should stay still. They all know it is better to be concealed that to move about when a helicopter is in the air.

The helicopter comes closer. Their fingers move nervously on safety catches, to go from lock to fire in an instant if they are spotted. They will have to fire furiously to suppress the door guns and cause maximum confusion so they can escape before the enemy responds effectively. Surprise, speed, and rapid fire will be the key to escape. A hundred rounds emptied into the side of the chopper ought to slow it down or make it swing away.

The whirling beat of chopper blades approaches the treetops. There is a rush and roar as it sweeps by just over their heads. Hiep thinks it would be tempting to fire a few rounds up through the bottom of the chopper. Whoever is sitting there would get a big surprise, courtesy of Ho Chi Minh. The chopper is going so fast over the trees that its occupants wouldn't know where the shots came from, but it would also be hard to hit even a large target that is available for only an instant. Besides, it would be suicidal to risk giving away their position so near the soldiers in the fort.

The five VC watch the chopper fly in a wide arc, circling back toward the fort. Then it quickly drops below the trees into the open area where the VC have a clear view. The chopper barely touches the ground as it hovers in the middle of the clearing. Out jump six men, most of them in American uniforms. One, who has the markings of a lieutenant, carries an M60 machine gun with bandoliers of gleaming brass bullets, maybe two hundred rounds, slung back over his shoulders. Another with the double bars of a captain holds an M16 as does the sergeant next to him, who also carries a radio on his back. Another sergeant has an M16 and medical bag. A fifth man, with sergeant's insignia, holds an M79 grenade launcher and has two cloth bandoliers around his chest. The last man is a Vietnamese sergeant, maybe an interpreter or some type of liaison between the ARVN and the Americans. The Americans look like a team of advisors, few men, all officers and NCOs, heavily armed, landing near an ARVN location.

The six invaders quickly spread out and hit the ground with their weapons ready. To Hiep they look primed for action and they mean business. He thinks, *I would not attack them unless I had at least a dozen men or more to overwhelm them, even without the helicopter and the ARVNs. Maybe another day.*

After the chopper dusts off, the six men hug the ground, looking for signs of attack. All is quiet for a moment. Then, there is a shout from the fort. A sentry stands up and waves his arms. The Americans wave back and begin moving toward the fort. Hiep thinks, no doubt this is a rendezvous that was planned, but maybe the communication between the Americans and the ARVN was not clear. The government troops should have notified the Americans that they occupy the fort and had secured the area; or maybe the Americans know the government troops are supposed to be there, but had little confidence in their ability. After all, we are right under their noses and could take a clear shot. That is a good reason to attach the advisors to the ARVN so they can communicate better with their support elements.

The five VC are ready to go. They know the arrival of the Americans will distract the sentries from the perimeter of the fort. They slowly back themselves over the jungle floor. Their movements can barely be seen as they only move their toes, and elbows and slide very slowly, hugging the ground as they inch into a dry stream bed that will conceal their departure.

———

Later that day, Hiep and Thanh sit under a thatched porch roof, each with a bowl of rice and fish cupped in one hand, a white ceramic spoon in the other hand. They eat slowly, savoring the Mekong Delta rice. Thin poles that rest on stones in the mud floor hold up the roof. The house is in a hamlet at the other end of the peninsula.

Thanh says, "This is the best rice in the country. We are fortunate to be assigned here."

Hiep pauses before taking a bite and says, "Some of the people here offer generous hospitality because they support our cause. I still like to offer a few piastres to share the burden."

"I agree," says Thanh.

It has taken them three hours, moving swiftly on the trails to cover the distance from the morning reconnaissance point. They had passed through several small hamlets and seen the occasional isolated houses where people waved meekly as they passed. The main trail also passed by graveyards marked with stones and small stone temples honoring ancestors. Here and there a palm tree had a flat spot carved out on the trunk where local VC had painted a red and blue flag with a white or gold star in the middle. Thanh is pleased to see the flags of resistance marking the area as VC domain.

Sitting up in his chair Thanh says, "The rockets we fire at Ben Tre must be having an effect on the American imperialists and the puppet government. They are worried; otherwise they would not send American advisors and the government battalion. The local people see we can bring force against the regime."

"Yes," says Hiep "we have been busy in the past few weeks and our work is paying off. We have built a force of more that one hundred men and women fighters."

Thanh nods and says, "Now that we have organized them into platoons and a better rocket squad, it is clear that they have more confidence and enthusiasm. There is a stronger identification with our mission. I think we have done well!"

Hiep smiles and adds, "We have done well but we are also lucky to organize such a force near Ben Tre where the Americans and government forces have such a strong influence."

"That is true," says Thanh. "We still have the big challenge to change the government's influence."

Hiep says, "In some ways it has been easy to motivate the fighters. Their families had fought the French or they had suffered under the government's corruption and tyranny. Some had a brother, sister, cousins, or parents who had been targeted by the Thieu regime for imprisonment or assassination. They are fighting for their family, for revenge, or justice. But, the local villagers, compared to the fighters, are different. They want to stay in their homes no matter who is in control of the area. Except for our dedicated supporters, there are people who do small favors for our fighters when they are around, but they may do the same for the government or Americans whenever they are in the area."

Thanh replies, "My friend, you are very observant. But don't worry, I think we will win the villagers' sympathies. They can see the gains we have made and many of them hate this American war."

Hiep responds, "You will have a chance to convince them tomorrow at the special meeting, my friend. You have a talent for persuading people."

"Thank you," says Thanh. "I think we can get their support in a friendly way with the power of our ideals. It is too bad that other comrades have resorted to violent methods in their areas of operation. That kind of news is more likely to turn people away from our cause."

Hiep nods his head slowly with a tight, flat grimace on his lips. In the back of his mind his thinks of stories he has heard about VC who used force and terror to persuade villagers to the communist way. There is the story about the recalcitrant hamlet chief near Danang who was mutilated in front of his wife, four children, and others. Then his wife and three children were tortured and killed, and only the five-year-old daughter was left, crying. There are stories of thousands of beheadings, throat slittings, and worse mutilations done to persuade the local population. Hiep thinks that he would not like to be part of that horror.

After pausing for a moment Hiep responds to Thanh, "For now it will be enough to have their compliance and quiet acquiescence. As long as the villagers do not run to the government, if they keep quiet about our activities, that will be enough cooperation for now. We will see how it goes tomorrow."

"Good," says Thanh, "but now we must plan to give Ben Tre another taste of the rockets. I think we need to make a diversion so our rocket squad can go safely across the land."

Hiep nods his head and shifts in his chair, saying, "We could send a strong force from the river on the north against the enemy's headquarters encampment, under the cover of night. How about a platoon reinforced with captured 60mm mortars? They could fire off a dozen mortar rounds at the invaders."

"That would be quite a diversion!" responds Thanh with enthusiasm in his voice. That should be enough to keep the invaders busy."

Hiep continues, "Scouts could go ahead of our main body to detect outlying listening posts and ambushes. They could either skirt them or deploy small rifle teams to interrupt and confuse the government troops while the main body presses its attack. Meanwhile the rocket squad will make its way across the peninsula on a trail well away from the battalion and fire half a dozen rockets on the American compound in Ben Tre. We can time the diversion to cover their retreat."

"I like your idea," says Thanh. "We have enough time to organize it for next week."

———

The next evening Thanh stands under a tree in a small hamlet on the outer peninsula, well into VC territory. A crowd of villagers gathers around him in a semicircle within a wide area between several thatched dwellings. The smell of cooking fires in concrete or mud ovens lingers in the air after the evening meal.

A few dozen people have arrived from nearby hamlets to hear this recent arrival from North Vietnam. A quiet murmur can be heard. An occasional soft laugh or exclamation rises from old acquaintances catching up on life events. They sit on logs and stools or stand casually, shifting their weight from one foot to the other, arms folded or hanging in comfortable positions.

Hiep stands quietly in the background occasionally nodding when he recognizes a familiar face. He smiles warmly when he sees one of the newly recruited fighters. He feels confident that the gathering will not be interrupted, knowing that a few seasoned fighters have stationed themselves in a protective circle on the outskirts of the hamlet. He hopes that he and Thanh can use friendly persuasion and a little patience to gain the support of these villagers. It is a good sign that there are so many fighters already here, and that Ben Tre has a long history of revolt against imperialists.

Thanh clears his throat. Many eyes turn toward him and an expectant silence grows in the late light of the day. Thanh outstretches his arms in an embracing way and smiles as he begins to speak. "My friends, my comrade Hiep and I are happy to see all of you."

Some turn to look at Hiep standing in the rear, leaning against a porch pole. He smiles broadly and waves.

Thanh clears his throat again. "Many thanks to you for coming here this evening. It is very good that the loyal families of the Huu Dinh can gather together to help protect their homeland from American imperialists and the puppet government in Saigon. My name is Nguyen Tat Thanh and I have been sent by our leaders in Hanoi with a message for you. The North supports you in your struggle against the tyrants and imperialists."

Thanh's voice drops slightly lower. "Our leaders know you are tired of the American war and the intrusions on your lives that it brings. The government moves happy families from their homes to their strategic hamlets that you do not want. They declare your homelands are free-fire zones and lay waste to your houses, your property, and your ancestral lands. Government troops invade quiet villages and mistreat the people, burn houses, and spoil your food stores. Innocent villagers have been hurt and killed by American bombs. This is not what the good people of Vietnam want for their families, their villages, the lands of their ancestors."

The people in the crowd are nodding their heads in affirmation and there are low grunts of assent. Thanh feels that he is connecting with the people and his confidence grows.

He continues with rising enthusiasm. "I have heard that you and your friends have suffered under the Saigon regime. They have removed many people from these hamlets, and they have fired their weapons into this area. You have been treated badly by government officials who favor their friends and steal supplies that are meant for you. You are not alone. All around Vietnam people like us have suffered these abuses for many years. Before, it was the imperialistic French and the Bau Dai regime. Then it was Diem who treated all but his friends badly. Now it is Thieu who continues to make our lives miserable."

Standing in the back Hiep sees that the crowd listens intently to Thanh. The night is still. He smiles inwardly with a growing appreciation for Thanh's knowledge and words.

Thanh pauses, and then continues. "I come from the north where Uncle Ho lives in Hanoi. He has fought long and hard against these abuses from foreigners. His aim is to unite all of Vietnam, North and South—like it was before the Western imperialists divided our country in 1954. Ho believes in our freedom and independence more than any other thing. In 1945 he declared Vietnamese independence but the allies thought the French were more important. Before that, in 1919 at Versailles, Ho tried to appeal to the American president, Woodrow Wilson, to support our self-determination without French domination, but the president ignored Ho. The Americans believe that independence only applies to them."

Thanh hears louder affirmations from the crowd and some people clearly nod their heads in agreement.

He says, "Even after we defeated the French at Dien Bien Phu in 1954, the west refused to recognize our independence. But, remember, we are a people who have been oppressed and abused by outside powers for a long time. Remember our brave heroes in the past: Tran Hong Dao who repelled the Mongols, Le Doi who repelled the Ming Dynasty, and Nguyen Hue who pushed out the Manchus. We have their example and their strength in our blood. We are patient and we can outlast our enemies. And now, things are changing."

Thanh pauses for a breath and continues, "Ho said that '...the Vietnamese people will suffer anything rather than renounce their freedom.' We will never give up fighting for our freedom and uniting our people. We have strongholds throughout the North and South. We support fighters with weapons, equipment, and food brought down the Truong Son Trail. It is not easy but we have many patriots, men and women, who make the long trip carrying supplies. Our enemies wear themselves down by constantly looking for our fighters, trying to bomb our supply lines and our homelands, but we fade away to safe areas and live to strike them again."

Thanh feels affirmative energy from the crowd and continues. "Now we are striking them in Ben Tre, the capital of their Kien Hoa province. We attacked them there during Tet in 1968 and now we are hitting them with rockets. They may fear another uprising like Tet. That is good because the Americans will see that their war is not working. All of their efforts go for very little gain. Even the people in the United States demonstrate against the war and see that it is senseless to keep on. In fact, we can see that the Americans are withdrawing troops, and now they are talking more of peace in Paris."

Thanh sees that some who were sitting are now standing, trying to catch every word.

Thanh pauses for effect, looks at the crowd, slowly draws a breath, and says, "With your help we can keep firing rockets at Ben Tre, and keep wearing down the government and the confidence of the Americans. We have dozens of fighters in this area. They need to know that they can pass safely through your hamlets without betrayal. They may need to rest in your houses. But most of all they need to know that you believe in what they are doing and that you admire their courage. Can you do that? Will you support our brave fighters?"

The crowd responds with clapping and many shouts of approval. Some say, "Yes," and some say they will help. Others smile and clap vigorously. There are some faces, though, that reveal indifference or fear.

Thanh says, "Thank you, my friends. We will continue our efforts, and you will see the collapse of this repressive government and the departure of the Americans. It may be a little difficult in the short term, but in the long run we will all be better. Thank you and good night to you."

The crowd disperses slowly, with many people shaking Thanh's hand. Hiep makes his way over to his comrade.

He says, "Well done, brother. You have won many friends tonight. There may be some who doubt us, but we can convince them with our success. For now we have more support for our rocket attacks on Ben Tre."

Ten

PUFF THE MAGIC DRAGON

Brad and I are with the battalion headquarters group and reserve company in a second fort, about a kilometer from the first fort where our MAT team had been inserted by chopper. We are still a few kilometers north of Ben Tre, which is well within range of VC rockets. Captain Blake and Sergeant Clarkson are with Alpha Company in a position forward of our right flank. Company B is forward of our left flank. Our plan is to sweep down the peninsula and force the VC out of the area.

The battalion commander is Thieu u ta (major) Tan, a middle-aged man of average height, with a wide face and a smile framed by slightly puffy cheeks. He is friendly and seems to be a competent military leader.

The reserve company of infantry troops is digging fighting positions around the perimeter of a central mound, a mud bunker that accommodates about a dozen men including the battalion commander, his staff, and us. Three rings of coiled concertina wire surround our position. The usual array of claymore mines is placed in the wire to repel enemy attackers. Our men like the claymores because they blast a killing zone with shrapnel out to fifty meters, giving more effect than firing rifles, and avoiding the telltale muzzle blasts that become enemy targets. Trip flares are placed around the wire to alert us to enemy attack at night. The old trick of hanging rattling, pebble filled, used C-ration cans on the barbed wire supplements the trip flares. At the sound of rattling pebbles or the flash of a flare, soldiers will set off a claymore and blow away intruders, be they VC or slithering pythons.

After the first night inside the fort, I wonder if I would rather sleep outside in the foxholes. The thick walls of the bunker are covered with a timber and mud roof, like a tunnel ceiling. We sleep in a cave-like room. The Vietnamese staff stretch out on wooden bunks, like shelves, next to the walls. Brad and I sling our net hammocks between roof support posts. I had thought this would be a cozy arrangement because I like swinging in the hammock, and we are well protected by the roof. Last night we had slathered ourselves with bug repellent in the usual way and looked forward to a good night's sleep, barring any interruptions from Victor Charles.

Unfortunately, last night I was awakened by something unpleasant that had fallen on my face. It was a creepy, crawly thing that made me grimace and wake up brushing my arms wildly over my face and body. Then I pulled out my flashlight and shined it up at the ceiling. It was covered with a legion of large, hard-shelled cockroaches scurrying about, pushing against each other, and knocking some down in their scrabbling haste. I watched them for a while with a fascinated disgust and the realization that the jungle is filled with all sorts of crawling, slithering creatures that I would not like to have as guests. Just like us, they are out here trying to survive.

By then Brad woke up and said, "That's the trouble with these mud holes. They attract bugs, rats, snakes, and who knows what other creatures."

We decided to put more bug lotion on our faces, fatigues, and the ropes on our hammocks. Then we put olive drab, bandana-like cloths over our faces and tried to go back to sleep.

It took me a while to drift off as I kept waiting for another roach to fall on my face cloth. Also, I was trying to decide which was worse, dying from an overdose of the chemicals in the bug lotion or going outside to risk a rocket or mortar attack. Considering the immediacy of death by projectiles and my own inertia I opted to stay put and take my chances with the critters.

With the first yellow glow of the rising sun filtering through the jungle canopy, Tieu u ta Tan is sending out platoons from Companies Alpha and Bravo to reconnoiter our path forward. Brad and I go with one of the reserve platoons to clear a large tract of land in the center of the peninsula. We don't think we will run into enemy squads, but booby traps are a real possibility. Our troops are setting dynamite charges on the palm trees to blow them down and make a clear line of sight through the middle of the peninsula. This is supposed to help us detect VC trying to cross over the land to rocket Ben Tre.

Some of the trees have flat spots cut into their trunks painted red and blue with a centered gold star. These are meant to show the local population that the VC rule the area. We are careful to watch for booby traps as we approach these trees and blow them up to show that the Republic of South Vietnam is in power. The trees fall in a crisscross pattern over the area that makes a confusing tangle of debris. I think this reflects the destruction and confusion of this crazy war. It seems to me that the local population might be swayed by the presence of the force that can raise its flag in the area, but I expect they only wish for peace and quiet to return to their homeland.

All day long the dynamite explodes and trees crash to the ground. Occasionally throughout the day wounded soldiers are carried back from the companies in front. They encounter squads of VC firing rifles or setting off booby trap explosives. Our soldiers carry their wounded buddies back in seats made of sticks or lying down on a poncho stretcher. Some are carried in farm carts and rolled back over the trails. Most of the wounds are light and we have no dead today.

A few wounded men are assembled in a small clearing along a dirt trail, an area secured by a platoon of the reserve company. The trail connects to the dirt road that runs back to the district town. We are not able to call in a medevac chopper because we are still clearing a space for a landing zone, so we plan to evacuate the wounded by vehicles sent in from district headquarters.

The Vietnamese officers are arranging for a jeep and trucks while Brad and I keep our headquarters at district advised of developments. Those drivers will earn every piastre of pay because they must eyeball every inch of the road to avoid road mines. Right now, a special unit is clearing as many mines as they can find. District arranges for the supply chopper, good old Ishmael 11, to fly over the road to detect enemy activity. A fort along the road sends out troops to secure the flanks of the road.

Brad and I are sitting in the shade of a coconut tree off to the side, watching Doc and the medics treat the wounded. We have our radio next to us to monitor the evacuation efforts and make calls when necessary. We talk during stretches of time between radio calls and the steps of the evacuation.

"Hey, Brad," I say with a quiet tone in my voice, waving my hand toward the wounded, "It's too bad good men are being wounded and killed in this war."

He looks up from checking the bullets in a magazine and says, "Yeah, but wadda ya mean?"

"I mean, the utilitarians say that right action leads to happiness and wrong action leads to unhappiness, but how can these guys be happy?"

Brad replies, "Yeah, they must be thinking pain and survival. Maybe later they will believe they made the right sacrifice to serve their country and will be happy, proud soldiers."

"Yeah, sure," I say, "but the VC think they are right too."

Brad replies, "More likely, someone is going to be unhappy in all of this, the wounded soldiers, the villagers caught in the middle of conflict, the defeated country. It's a puzzle."

"Yeah," I say. "Maybe doing the right thing is not about taking sides; it's about doing right for everybody, doing the right thing together."

"Maybe we should be sure we are right before we get into a war, LT. Who knows in this war?"

"If we're not right about this war, then...our men are wounded or killed for the wrong reason. The longer this Nam thing goes on, the less it means. The cosmic calculus just doesn't solve the equation here."

I reach behind my back and pull the canteen out of its canvas pouch, then look at Brad as he clears his throat.

He says, "LT, it's too deep, deeper than the Delta mud in the rainy season."

"Hey, Brad, you're the philosopher. I thought you liked deep stuff."

"OK, LT, I think you make sense. You're saying mankind can't do right when they are at war, killing each other, unless there is a justifiable reason, right?"

"Yep, I say. "Self-defense would be a good reason. Otherwise it's endless, spiraling, futility for mankind... unremitting futility. Look at history. Are we doomed to futility?"

Brad replies, "I don't know. It's hard to see the answer in the purple haze. But one thing I know for sure, like John Stuart Mill said, 'War is an ugly thing.'"

"Right," I reply, unscrewing the top of my canteen.

Brad looks with satisfaction at the gleaming brass bullets he puts back in his magazine and stuffs it in the bandolier slung over his chest. He says, "LT, too much thinking right now may not be healthy."

I look at Brad and nod before taking a long drink from the canteen.

Brad says, "You know LT, the good news right now is that, so far, we have not seen any VC atrocities here. I'm worried it could get nasty for the locals. Last tour, I saw some bad stuff done to villagers. I heard that Charlie had committed over one hundred thousand acts of terror against the South Vietnamese. One fanatical VC tortured and decapitated his own fifteen-year-old sister for giving information to American soldiers, and another cut out the tongues of his wife and two children for cooperating with marines."

Brad pauses and with glazed eyes looks at the trees across the clearing. He says. "It is amazing that our peace protestors do not mention the atrocities when they say we are fighting noble revolutionaries. I don't think George Washington tortured and mutilated his adversaries."

As I grimace at this statement Brad says, "On the other hand, we know Thieu's government isn't very pure either."

"You're right," I reply. "We've heard of their bombing innocent villagers, forcing relocations, government corruption...hardly true virtue."

"Yeah," Brad says, but right now the bad news for us is that these Charlies really want to kill us and our men. Who knows what they will do to the locals?"

"Uh huh. They sure haven't surrendered yet," I say.

Brad has a right to be concerned. He carries a lot of bad memories in his head. He doesn't talk much about it, but I believe he had personally witnessed some nasty stuff on his last tour in Nam. Last night he was talking and twitching in his sleep and almost rolled out of his hammock. I think that working with the lien doi out here in the bush with regular enemy contact is bringing back old memories. He has a few demons.

Even back at Firebase Bravo I noticed that Brad had a few bad nights. After a contact with Charlie the rest of us would celebrate with a few beers and debrief the events back at the hooch, but Brad seemed uneasy on those occasions. Sometimes he would take a few swigs on a bottle of Lord Walker Scotch to help him sleep. He was never unfit for action, but I think he just needs to dull the mental anguish. Being as smart as he is, I think he just knows more than most of us about how bad things can get. The bad experiences penetrate deeply.

He doesn't have a bottle out here, but he can sure get loose back at the compound in Ben Tre. I'm not worried though, he is always ready when needed.

———

This evening, we are back in the same mud bunker with the cockroaches. It is dark in the surrounding jungle. A dim kerosene lamp casts a feeble light on the mud walls and timbers. The dull yellow light is a luxury in this dark hole. It is even possible to make out the features on my field map.

We swing in our hammocks a few hours after enjoying a pleasant meal shared with Thie u ta Tan and his staff. The Major treated us to a chopped duck and vegetables over rice. His cook just cut the duck up into cubes about the size of a marshmallow and boiled them in a big pot with the greens. The major's cook and his helper carry the ducks on their shoulders in cages strung on a bamboo pole. There are maybe a half-dozen ducks to be relished one-by-one during the long weeks of the campaign. There is little chance for resupply of fresh poultry so the cook has to take good care of his food stores.

The dinner was a cut above whatever we can usually scrounge—a small can of chili, a can of C-rations that we dump over a cup of rice purchased from some local mamasan, if we are lucky. The problem is that we can't carry much in our little web packs for our field duty with the battalion. Our radio, weapons, and ammunition take up most of our load, and we need to travel light so we can easily consult our maps, compasses, and radio codebooks.

The major was quite proud of his ability to treat us to a nice meal and we were glad for something different. We smiled and nodded our heads and asked Sergeant Sang, our interpreter, to convey our thanks and appreciation. I tried to pick pieces that had some appeal from the common bowl while avoiding the remaining undistinguishable duck parts. While we were eating I looked over to the surviving ducks in their cages and wondered about their impending doom. How many tomorrows did they have? Then I thought, "How many tomorrows do we have?"

As we are lying in our hammocks we savor the pleasant fullness of a good meal and the quiet security of our encampment. The eleven bravos, code for infantrymen, in our reserve company are in their foxholes and have checked the concertina wire around our protective perimeter. The jungle bugs sing out in a constant chorus.

The peace and quiet of the evening is interrupted by an urgent sounding call on our field radio from Spooky, a gunship with mounted miniguns:

"Roughneck Three Five, Roughneck Three Five, this is Spooky."

I grab the handset and say, "This is Roughneck Three Five." Meanwhile, I'm thinking he can't see us but he knows we are operating in this area. How did he get my call sign?

"This is Spooky. We are over your AO with night surveillance gear. We have your location from your headquarters. We see approximately twenty-five enemy in combat formation approaching your position from the north and request permission to fire minis into your AO."

The hair stands up on the back of my neck as I feel an almost electric jolt in my brain. I suck in a shallow breath.

"This is Roughneck Three Five, roger, hold one, over."

I'm thinking, holy cow, those minis will tear up every square inch of our area. We have troops out on night patrol. Trung si Sang and Brad are nearby and have heard the call.

I point up at the gunship and say, "Trung Si Sang, tell the major we have night eyes up there and twenty five enemy are approaching our position. Ask where he has men out and get positions on the map. Ask if he can pull the men back and authorize firing."

There is a hurried discussion between Sang and the Vietnamese officers and a rapid exchange of gestures and words over the maps. I look at my own map to check that our targets are in a free fire zone where civilians are not living.

Sang points to a spot on the map and says, "Truong uy, we have ambush units over here, but they will clear them out in fifteen minutes."

"Good," I say.

We all know that it is easier to stop an assault with mini guns than with a few ambushes.

"Spooky, Spooky, this is Roughneck Three Five, over."

"This is Spooky, go ahead."

"This is Roughneck Three Five. We have units in that area but will withdraw in fifteen mikes so you can fire, over."

"Roughneck, this is Spooky. Roger, we will be back in fifteen mikes and call you for the all clear to fire, over."

"This is Roughneck Three Five, Roger. Good copy. Out."

Meanwhile, the battalion officers have already radioed their units to clear away from the designated coordinates. They have also put our perimeter defense company on full alert for a possible attack. I try to recall exactly what Spooky is and remember my training. Spooky is an AC-47 airplane, a military version of the venerable DC-3, which has mounted miniguns and the ability to provide close air support to infantry, even from three thousand feet up. Spooky has earned the admiration of the many troops it has saved from ground assault by overwhelming forces and is fondly called "Puff, the Magic Dragon." I am glad that we had figured a few hundred yards clearance from the target zone knowing that a lethal gunship firestorm at night is not guaranteed 100 percent accurate.

The Vietnamese officers like the idea of Spooky because they are not eager to have a concentrated VC force confront their ambushes. The VC know the area better than we do and the force may be much larger than Spooky had estimated, or there may be other forces not detected by Spooky, headed right for our battalion headquarters position. Even with the upper hand our squads would lose many men by opting for an ambush. Even worse, in the dead of night we might lose men to friendly fire. Better to let the gunship do its work.

We wait for our soldiers to withdraw from their positions. Things are pretty quiet at the moment. The bugs are singing loudly in the jungle.

Brad says, "LT, you can cut the tension with a knife."

"Yeah."

So now the die is cast. We hope that the VC attackers will not get wise to the gunship. If it is flying high enough maybe Charlie won't hear it. Even without much warning, the VC can react very quickly. They may have covered spider holes that they can dive into if it is a regular route of travel for them. Our Vietnamese officers smoke cigarettes, being careful to conceal the glowing tips behind the mud walls. The major sits patiently, looking over his map, conveying a calming effect to his men.

The radio cracks, even at low volume.

"Roughneck Three Five, Roughneck Three Five, this is Spooky. We are ready to rock and roll. What is your status, over?"

"This is Roughneck Three Five. We have all units pulled back to grid 659352. Do not fire into that grid. Fire north of that grid. I say again, fire north of grid 659352, over."

"This is Spooky, I copy fire north of grid 659352. Do we have permission to fire, over?"

"This is Roughneck Three Five, affirmative, you do have permission to fire, over."

"This is Spooky, roger, stand by, out."

There is a pause as I take a deep breath. Then the night lights up. Swirling streams of red tracers shower down on the treetops. The fickle fingers of fate are raining death and destruction with thousands of 7.62mm NATO rounds in full view of our position. The firing is so intense that it sounds like a high-pitched whirlwind. This is the closest thing to a tornado that I have experienced. The Vietnamese officers exchange wide-eyed looks of amazement. The knowing looks suggest that no one believes the VC can survive this torrent of bullets. Then, the deadly stream of firing stops abruptly. All is quiet. Even the bugs are silent. We wait. The officers call on their radios for reports from their units in the field.

One of the Vietnamese staff lieutenants looks at me wide-eyed, mouth half agape, and then he says, "Choy oi! Beaucoup boom, boom! Co van my number one, number one!" This more or less means Wow! Lots of firing and noise. American advisor is number one.

I meet his gaze and smile saying, "Cam on. VC beaucoup dinky dau. Xin loi VC!" This is my rough Vietnamese for, Thanks. The VC are crazy. I'm sorry about firing you up, Charlie.

The lieutenant gives me a broad smile, and says, "VC beaucoup dinky dau!"

"Roughneck Three Five, this is Spooky, this is Spooky, over."

"This is Roughneck Three Five, over."

"This is Spooky. We are done, can see no activity on target, over."

"This is Roughneck Three Five, What is your estimate of enemy KIA? Over."

"This is Spooky, maybe one KIA or WIA. We do not see anything else, over."

"This is Roughneck Three Five, roger. Thank you for your help Spooky, over."

"Roger Three Five, this is Spooky returning to base to refuel and reload. Good Luck Three Five. Spooky out."

We stand around the radios talking about the incident. We think that the VC must have jumped into covered positions before Spooky could adjust fire on the full target. Even if we got more of them the remaining VC will drag the bodies away before we can get there. Also, they may return to the site and ambush any of our men who come to investigate. The major decides not to send out any patrols to check the area this night. This is one of things I like about him. He is disciplined and cautious when it makes sense. Brad calls in a report to district.

An hour later we get a radio call from Major Hyde at our district headquarters. He says that Ben Tre is being attacked by rockets. Can we detect any VC activity on the south side of the peninsula? We have a few listening posts in that area but they report no sign of enemy activity. I think Charles must have gone around our units to avoid any contact, if their mission was to rocket Ben Tre. There is also a similar report from Captain Blake who is with Alpha company forward of our position on the south side. We relay this report this to Major Hyde. It is no surprise that the VC know exactly where we are and can maneuver at will. I wonder if the attack from the north was simply a diversion.

Brad says, "The look on your face says you aren't happy."

"Yep, I'm thinking that Mister Charles outfoxed us. He might not have enough forces for a full-scale attack on our battalion but he can distract our attention and cause a lot of damage. That gives him enough of a diversion to keep us busy while he pounds Ben Tre. It could be that Charles got the best of us even with all our fancy equipment and firepower, not to mention a sizable force of men. So, Brad, what does all your NCO experience tell you about how we deal with this?"

He pulls out a crumpled pack of Lucky Strikes, shakes one up, and sticks it between his lips. I flick my Zippo and he draws the flame quickly. He inhales and, after a pause, lets out the smoke. "Thanks for the light, LT. Maybe we need to realize that Charlie is always going to know more about the situation, weather, and terrain than we will. Maybe we need a better plan and need to get more aggressive."

After a pause, inhaling and exhaling smoke, the tip of the cigarette glowing brightly, Brad continues, "You know, it kind of reminds me of old Sun Tzu."

I'm glad we are concealed behind the mud wall so any lurking Charlies won't blow Brad's head off while he is taking a drag. "You mean that Chinese warrior who wrote *The Art of War*?"

"Yep, he was a master," says Brad. "He measured five things to assess the situation...the way, the weather, the terrain, the leadership, and discipline. Knowledge is the key to winning. It is more important to undermine enemy plans and ruin their alliances than to attack them. It seems the VC are doing that to us here. They fooled us and won the day. Every failure undermines our alliance with the South Vietnamese at some level."

"Makes sense, Brad. I think the 'way' is a very important part of it?"

"Yeah, it means getting people thinkin' the same way as the leaders, with the same goals."

"Yeah, we don't have that back home, and the South Vietnamese don't have it here."

Brad takes another drag on the cigarette with a thoughtful look in his eyes, and replies, "Our national leaders are not thinking like Sun Tzu, and their plans reflect that. We have our politicians confusing our generals, and the people of our country are confused and angry about this war. Plus, our resources are stretched half way around the globe. We are fighting on our enemy's homeland with many soldiers who are trying to avoid the draft and just plain don't give a damn. So we are not fighting this thing by Sun Tzu's book."

I look at Brad with respect, trying to take in all that he has expressed. The Sun Tzu stuff makes sense to me and I make a mental note to re-read the book.

"Brad," I say, "I can see that you have had this on your mind for a while. You make a lot of sense to me. But, what can we do right here, and right now?"

He says, "Our guys have good leadership and discipline and they know how to deal with the weather. A disadvantage is they are not familiar with the terrain of the Huu Dinh. But, a big question is, which do the villagers believe is better, our way or Charlie's way?

After reflecting for a moment, I say, "You're right, we could try to strengthen our approach on winning over the local people. That might help get them over to our way and strengthen their allegiance. We might gain an edge over Charles."

The next morning we get orders from Major Hyde to meet a chopper at a secure landing zone we had just cleared for future medevacs. It will pick us up for a meeting back at province headquarters. I think that the Colonel is spitting mad about the attack and wants to know how we let the VC slip through to pommel his headquarters with rockets. No doubt Major Hyde is under pressure to get better results.

Besides the prospects of a shower and a hot meal, the thought of going to the relative security of the province headquarters compound reminds me of R&R. I want to find out if my orders are still on track to meet Cathy in Hawaii in two weeks. She and I have been making plans for months for this seemingly impossible respite. Plans are made, things happen, and maybe it all works out. My mind cannot quite grasp the possibility of reunion with her; going from the bullets, mines, mud, heat and hostility of the VC to the streets of Waikiki to meet the woman of my life and future when the dragons are clawing at my back. It's a crazy world.

Eleven

PEOPLE LIKE US

Hiep and Thanh are pleased with the rocket attack on Ben Tre. They sit in a thatched house sipping tea with several VC platoon leaders discussing the events of the previous night. They are all dressed in the usual black, pajama-like shirts and pants. All agree that the local VC fighters accomplished the entire operation with enthusiasm and skill. The sun drops in the west, giving a warm orange-yellow glow to the sky before dusk. The assembled leaders go over each part of the mission and discuss it in detail to see if anything can be done better the next time.

The diversionary force of thirty fighters had slipped up the river in small boats. As planned, they had moved toward the known position of the government force headquarters, and carefully probed for pickets and listening posts or other government troop activity. They were prepared to make a quick, vigorous attack on the enemy force to inflict heavy damage and then withdraw quickly. They hoped to catch the government troops off guard and to divert their attention from the movement of the rocket squad. They also set up booby traps to make casualties of pursuing troops. Meanwhile the rocket squad carried two rocket launchers and ten rockets to a favorable firing position across from Ben Tre. The firing of the rockets was coordinated for the same time as the diversion.

The assessment of the men sitting in the house is that the overall plan worked out very well, except for some casualties among the fighters. The diversionary force had been half way from the river when one of the fighters heard the faint drone of an airplane overhead. The entire unit had frozen in place and listened, sweat in their hair, barely breathing, in silence. To some it seemed there was a foreboding disturbance in the air as if a giant dragon were flying overhead. The platoon leader suspected that any night flyer would have special surveillance equipment that would detect movement, so the entire unit hid in nearby covered fighting positions, in place from earlier operations.

The keen senses of the attackers and the cunning of their leader were rewarded with their very survival. Tongues of flame swept down upon them from the dragon above. The enemy tracers licked the surface of the jungle floor, tore up the treetops, and shredded the brush. A bullet in the head killed one of the fighters who didn't make it to a spider hole in time. The firing was so intense that it even penetrated some of the protective covers made of sturdy poles and thick mud. Two more suffered wounds to their extremities. After the torrent of fire the entire force of attackers retreated to the river carrying their dead and wounded with them. Hasty booby traps were set by those skilled with grenades and trip wires. They were all grateful for the keen senses and quick action that saved most of the force. They also speculated that the main object of the diversionary force had been accomplished, giving the rocket squads a good chance to carry out their mission.

Reports from spies in Ben Tre said that eight of the ten rockets had hit planned targets. The government's headquarters was hit in several places. A jeep and building-top radio equipment had been destroyed at the advisors compound, a round hit the helipad, and several hit the top of the joint Vietnamese and American command center, causing minor damage even with the heavy layer of sandbags. Shrapnel wounded one Vietnamese soldier.

The last light of the setting sun glows faintly through the window. With it reflecting on his high forehead, Thanh looks at Hiep and the other leaders, and then says, "We showed the puppet soldiers and their American allies that we can strike them, and hurt them, no matter what forces they have. They have a whole battalion in the Huu Dinh and they have air power. We can still hit their headquarters in Ben Tre."

"Yes, comrade," says Hiep, "and we have proved our endurance and capability to the people who live here. More people will believe in us and support us."

The platoon leaders finish their tea and with heads nodding they shake hands as they depart to their various hamlets.

After a few moments of quiet, Hiep looks at Thanh and says, "My friend, we have success like this all over the country. It makes me wonder why the Americans don't go away? We have killed many of them, we remain in areas they have cleared, and the people hate the American war."

"Yes, my friend," replies Thanh, "our history shows that we have always repelled invaders, no matter who, the Chinese, the Japanese, or the French. We had the will to decisively defeat the French at Dien Bien Phu in 1954, thanks to the brilliant leadership of Vo Nguyen Giap and the determination of our countrymen. We will ultimately prevail over the Americans and the South Vietnamese government too. We are fighting for our homeland."

Hiep nods his head several times in assent.

Thanh continues. "If the Americans knew us better they never would have invaded our country. They don't know that all we want is national unity and an end to the corruption and oppression of governments run by people like Diem, Bau Dai, and Thieu. No, it is the politicians of America and France who have wanted to invade our country. If the ordinary people of America knew our story, they might see that people like us are people like them."

"What we are doing is like their own revolutionary war, but they don't see it," says Hiep scratching his head with one hand through his thick, black hair.

Thanh replies, pupils expanded in his wide-apart eyes, "They are told we are communists because we have turned to communist governments for help. They put us in an ideological box and don't see us as people like themselves. They are too blind to reality, too afraid of communism, and their leaders are too set in their ways to leave us alone."

Thanh pauses, leans forward a bit and says emphatically, but quietly, "My friend, they will not pull out soon."

The two men sit on stools in the dark house, with only the dim light from a few glowing coals in the cooking fire. They listen as a breeze ruffles the thatch of the roof as if it is whispering a message.

After taking a sip of tea from his glass cup Thanh says, "You know, the Americans are very foolish; they don't even follow the advice of their own heroes. General

Douglas Macarthur warned them to avoid a large land war in Asia. They have their ideas about containing communism and the so-called domino theory. Rather than seek to understand us, they want to contain us or kill us. They are so confused they cannot see clearly. It is odd that the United States, which is built on the principles of freedom and the right to vote, ignored the 1955 elections that were promised to us after the Geneva Peace Conference. The elections were never held."

Hiep nods his head and responds with concern in his voice, "Thanh, my friend, you have learned many things from your schooling in Hanoi. It is a sad history we have. All of my life I have lived in a small village. I do not have the education given to you by Uncle Ho, but I do know how the people feel. Even if they believe in our cause there is great concern over the destruction of our homeland and the suffering of families. It would be enough for most farmers and poor people to be free of this constant conflict. They just want the fighting to stop. The people in the hamlets and villages just want a normal life, to raise their families, to grow their crops, to go to the market, to be happy. Instead they are caught up in the turmoil of power groups, political confusion, government programs, and puppet leaders."

Thanh sighs empathically and says, "Yes, the people suffer much from this conflict. At this very time the Huu Dinh has been invaded by government forces and Americans. Soldiers now occupy the lands of the villager's ancestors. Even the trees are blown up by the government troops. The invaders have altered the landscape so it is no longer like the memories of people who have lived here all of their lives. Their world is being destroyed. This is not the fault of villagers and simple people. The truth is that larger forces of history have changed our lives. Now things have gone too far to end without more fighting."

"When will we be free of this agony?" asks Hiep.

"My friend," says Thanh, "we will be free only when we pay the price of freedom. If our enemies will not understand us, if they will not respect us, if they will not leave us to pursue our own way of life, then we must stand up and we must prevail over them."

The two men look at each other with their jaws set and their eyes showing a renewed sense of purpose. Their minds are filled with visions of victory, their hearts swell with patriotic purpose, and they feel that their hands are strong enough to carry out the tasks ahead of them.

As the night grows darker and wind blows more briskly over the thatch, they continue their discussion. They agree that they must step up attacks against the government troops and their American advisors. They plan to set more mines in the road from the district town, set more booby traps along trails, and use their forces to snipe at advancing troops but only attack enemy units in force when there is an advantage.

Hiep straightens up on his stool and says, "These are good plans, my friend. I am eager to make them happen."

Shifting in his seat, Thanh smiles and replies, "Our countrymen have prevailed in the past against larger forces and we can do it here in the Huu Dinh."

Twelve

DANCING WITH THE DEVIL

After our brief recall to province, we are driving a jeep down the only road in the Huu Dinh on our way to the new lien doi command post. It is the third fort occupied by our forces during this campaign, a few kilometers east of the second fort. The headquarters group had advanced to it following Alpha and Bravo Company's maneuvers during our three days away.

The new headquarters fort is on the edge of the clearing where we had previously collected our wounded for evacuation. It is a town square of sorts, a place where trails converge and widen out with a few thatched houses around it. The triangular mud fort occupies one side of the square. It is less run down and taken over by jungle than the others we have occupied. The occupation of the fortification shows villagers that we have advanced to a strong point well within territory previously dominated by VC.

So far, Mr. Charles has been pushed almost half way down the peninsula. We have dynamited trees and occupied old forts to secure captured territory. Resistance has been light with only a few booby traps and sporadic fire from small enemy squads. Most of the booby traps had been discovered before inflicting damage. Less than a dozen of our men have been wounded and evacuated safely to district town. We believe we have wounded several VC since the night fire with Spooky claimed one possible enemy KIA. Since then, we captured one VC and sent him to the rear for interrogation by intelligence experts.

The road is hardpacked dry mud so only occasional flares of dust spin off from our jeep tires. There are six passengers. Captain Blake sits in the right front commander's seat, the polished pistol grips of his twin .45 caliber automatics revealed slightly by the polished black, custom leather holsters on each side. Brad drives, his eyes peeled on the road ahead searching for signs of a road mine. Doc and I are sitting atop sand bags on the rear fenders with Trung Si Sang and Clarkee between us on the rear seat, also covered with sand bags. In fact, sand bags line every possible place on the floor or seats of the jeep, a small comfort given our fear of an explosion from underneath. Even though our allies clear the roads by day, Charlie sets new traps by night. Maybe the sand bags will save our lives, or maybe just half our lives with a few missing limbs or paralysis.

Our eyes move from the road ahead to the tree lines a football field distance away on either side. We all know this is the same road where Captain Brown and Sergeant Johnson were blown away when their jeep hit a mine. We remember hearing the whole incident reported over the field radio by the eyewitness account of Ishmael 11, our supply chopper pilot. A voice in my head says, *This is not a training exercise. If you don't pay attention you will get blown away!*

Even as my senses are focused on the road and tree line, a dull, gloomy memory sits in the back of my mind. Under a numbing shroud I recall an experience from our few days back at province headquarters where we had been summoned to review the rocket attack on Ben Tre and plan our next moves. While there, we were informed that First Lieutenant Finerman and Sergeant First Class Barnes, members of MAT 17, had been killed by a booby trap while on patrol with their popular force platoon. They had passed a VC flag painted on a tree where they also saw a cluster of four or five telltale red mackerel cans made into homemade grenades.

As reported by their interpreter, Lieutenant Finerman had stopped to investigate as Sergeant Barnes warned him to stay away and try instead to blow the booby traps from a distance. When the Lieutenant persisted in checking out the explosives Sergeant Barnes walked over to him just when the whole thing blew up, sending shrapnel into their heads, chests, arms, and legs. They both died instantly.

Since we were back in the rear, we were able to attend a service for the two men. We don't often get to pay our respects to fallen members of our province team, so this was something we could do to help deal with this loss and the accumulated, unremitting sorrow of previous losses.

The ceremony was held under the open-air pavilion, between several buildings in the middle of the concrete walled compound. An American flag hung at the end of the structure where two rifles were pushed, bayonets first, into the ground in front of the flag. Helmets were placed on the butts of the vertical rifles and boots were placed on the ground in front of the rifles. A chaplain said a few words about the courage, loyalty, and sacrifice of these two good men. He also said, "Their sacrifice will not be forgotten." I do not forget their sacrifice, especially since it could have been me; but I do think the average American will never fully appreciate what it means to face giving your life for your country. How will those who send others to protect their freedom in blood remember the soldiers who served and fell in the line of duty?

As the chaplain spoke, my mind raced with the question of why they didn't follow the protocol to blow the explosive trap up with a time delay charge. Did they think they were immortal? I know that despite all the rules for safety, a situation like this is tempting. It is hard to pull yourself away from the deadly intrigue of an enemy's trap in plain view. Your enemy is taunting you through the flag painted on the tree and explosives in plain sight. You know Charles was right there in this spot. It is a dare. You think that if you are smart enough to see it, then you are smart enough to defuse it. Then you are dead.

After the chaplain spoke, the dozen or so of us arose from the wooden benches, walked to a point beside the displayed rifles and boots. Each in turn, we stepped in front of the display representing Lieutenant Finerman, came to full attention and saluted; then stepped in front of the display representing Sergeant Barnes, came to full attention, and saluted again. Each move was done with military precision: two steps forward, right face, salute, left face, two steps forward, right face, salute, left face, two steps forward out of the hallowed space. The precision reflected the grief and grim respect for our fallen team members that we felt on this somber occasion.

As the jeep bumps and jolts in the ruts of the road these memories do not completely divert my attention. Mostly they are a gauzy, aching presence in the back of my mind while my eyes search for present danger. Occasionally, the memories do sharpen into focus, only for a moment to recall a vivid picture of the funeral with resonant feelings of sadness and dejection, but I fight to keep my attention on guard.

We keep looking for any sign of disturbance on the road surface. It could be a newly dug area, or an upright spike that is the trigger for a mine beneath the surface. Then we see a jeep coming from the other direction. It slows, and then stops only one hundred and fifty feet in front of us. The passenger signals for us to stop and then gets out. He walks to a spot on the road half way between the two vehicles and stares down at the road. He stoops and looks closely at a spot where there is a spike protruding from the ground. We can see that it looks like a mine. He uses a bayonet to scrape dirt away from the spike and away from an antitank mine big enough to blow us all sky high. He puts a pin in the mine to keep it from exploding and waves us forward.

The man is a Vietnamese major who had been sent to confer with our battalion commander. He waves us around to indicate that he will stay and deal with the mine. We stop momentarily to thank him and offer assistance. He declines, but is clearly quite pleased that he discovered the mine. We are all in awe of his skill in finding the mine and probably saving our lives. If we had been a minute earlier we might have saved him or maybe we would have been blown to pieces.

We arrive at the village square and pull up in front of the fort. Thie u ta Tan is there directing operations.

There are two motorcycle carts with two or three of our wounded soldiers in each. One is lying down on the bottom of the cart, his leg field dressed, blood oozing from the strips of bandage. Another is slumped against the back of the cart, his arm in a bloody bandage. The other cart contains three soldiers, lightly wounded in the head and arms. At a glance I see that the wounds look like they were caused by a booby trap.

I walk over to the wounded men and raise my hand in a greeting. The upright soldiers smile and nod, their eyes showing they are glad for this recognition. I know the Vietnamese word for wounded. "Bithuong!" I say while gesturing toward their bloodied bodies. One replies, "VC Number ten, Truong uy." I reply, "You number one." I walk to the cart with the prostrate soldier. His eyes are open. He is weak but his wounds appear to be nonfatal. "You number one," I say. He smiles very faintly. Then the cycolo drivers kick over their engines, and the medevac carts slowly pull away across the square to the road.

I say, "Brad, the fighting will get tougher now. Charlie has been driven down the peninsula and he's getting crowded. He'll push back hard."

Brad grunts an assent as Captain Blake walks over from his talk with Thie u ta Tan.

Blake says, "As you can see, we are getting into more contact now. Those wounded came from an advance this morning. Two companies are operating forward on parallel tracks to flush out VC. There are booby traps everywhere. VC squads are doing harder hit-and-run against our platoons. It looks like they have stepped up action against us."

I reply, "Maybe they don't like us blowing down their VC flag trees and getting in the way of their attacks on Ben Tre."

"Yeah," says Blake, "We have a job to do, but we won't get it done before you go on R&R.

"That's OK," I say. "It will be nice to have something to come back to.

"Ha," he says.

Meanwhile, I am thinking, *It's hard to believe, soon I will leave for Hawaii and my sweet Cathy. Better watch my step.*

We have planned R&R for months, the subject of regular letters between Cathy and me. She has made all the arrangements: her plane ticket, the Kahala Hilton. Our longing to be together could only be expressed in those flimsy little airmail envelopes that cross thousand of miles of ocean and land. But R&R is a luxury I cannot dwell on too long. There are too many things in the way of getting there. Too many VC, too many nights in the jungle, too many bullets and booby traps. Any of these could cut short the dreams of getting away from it all, of reuniting with my wife, of getting a taste of the world.

It is too hard to imagine what the shock would be like to Cathy if she arrives in Hawaii to find that I am not there, a sudden casualty lost in the abyss between two worlds. Hers, a normal, regular life full of love for our little daughter, family, friends, trips to the grocery store, traffic, the town, all the usual things of life back in the USA. And there is the other world that holds me in its wicked web, a violent world, where death and the devil are encountered at every turn, where enemies lurk in unexpected places, where life is a constant military operation, where fear underlies every experience, where every day begins with a question mark.

If I wind up in a body bag for R&R, that would be a terrible twist of fate. It is a ticket to ride back home where the ticket price takes everything you have, a devilish proposition, a freakish welcome for my wife waiting in Hawaii. If I arrive in one piece, my body and soul may be intact but my mind carries the brutality and craziness of the jungle world that bends my sense of humor and saps the joy from good experiences. These things might be held down and pushed to the back of my mind for a few days with the thrill of meeting my love in Hawaii. I must contain these things so they do not contaminate her world or mar the joy of our reunion.

It is night now. Brad and I are sitting on our hammocks strung between poles in the corner of the fort. I relish the pleasure of smoking a stogie as Brad looks up at the smoke rings from his Lucky Strike. The radios squelch on and off on the other side of the room. Thie u ta Tan and his staff exchange messages with troops sent forward in the jungle. We have already checked in with Captain Blake, Doc, Sergeant Clarkson, and Sergeant Sang who have gone out with a forward company and are now set up in a night defensive position.

We are a vital radio link with district headquarters and the firepower needed to deal with an attack. Without Sang, Brad and I must rely on our limited Vietnamese, a few French words, and the ability of these officers to speak some English to support our team members and allies. We have a solid radio contact with the district advisory staff. Very reassuring.

Brad lightly pushes his booted feet against the hard-packed mud of the floor and swings in his hammock. "You may be right LT, we may be doomed to a futilitarian existence. Today, our guys were wounded and hurting, and Mr. Charles almost blew us away on the road. The pain and suffering doesn't stop."

"Yeah, Brad. It's the devil's day."

Brad says, "The devil is happy. The colonel isn't happy, LBJ isn't happy, Nixon isn't happy. Who here is happy? GIs who died here are not happy. I don't think the VC are happy. Maybe you're right. The only way to happiness is the common good. No war!"

"Brad, you're going philosophical tonight...There must be a reason we keep having this conversation. If it makes you feel any better, I carry around this John Stewart Mill quote that gives me some rationale for what we are doing. If we are defending the peace in specific situations, like the Huu Dinh, it gives me a shred of hope"

I pull the quote out of my pocket, take it out of its plastic wrapper, and read it aloud:

> The person who has nothing for which he is willing to fight, nothing which is more important than his own personal safety, is a miserable creature and has no chance of being free unless made and kept so by the exertions of better men than himself.

"What do you think, Brad?"

He replies, "I like that. You think we can do some good in our small area of operations?"

"Yeah. We can only deal with our small part. If Charlie is bombing Ben Tre, or harming the local people, then we are like the sheriff trying to bring law and order. If we can do something right, even in the turmoil of the larger picture, then it helps me make the best of a bad situation."

In a hopeful tone Brad says, "Yeah, maybe we can do a little good here even if this whole big war is questionable."

"Right," I say. "Our politicians and their allies are fumbling, they don't learn from the past. All the smart people in the Washington power structure can't seem to agree. They are caught up in misguided sincerity, or worse, while we are out in the bush. The fickle finger of fate is pointing at us, Brad. It's futile. But maybe in certain parts there are just situations. We can deal with the devil we know."

"It's a kind of desperate attempt to deal with craziness, isn't it?" says Brad.

"Yeah, it helps keep your soul intact when you are dancing with the devil. I wouldn't say this in front of just anybody. You know, we have to keep a stiff upper lip. But we know each other well enough, so we can talk about it. Also, we don't know everything. Maybe there is some secret reason why this war is right. Right now, for us, we'll do our duty because trying to do some little thing right is a matter of honor... and sanity."

"You're right," says Brad. "We're just a couple of loyal futilitarians struggling to find the right way, dancing with the devil."

"That's what it feels like, Brad, dancing with the devil."

"Yeah," says Brad. "Do our part right. Do all the stuff the army taught us to stay alive. Get through the day. Get through the night. Fight the good fight."

"Brad, it's amazing how you can go from philosophical to poetical practicality in a flash."

"Yeah, like a muzzle flash," says Brad.

"Works for me," I say, lying back in the hammock netting, dropping my hand down to my open boot containing the .357 magnum to make sure it is within easy reach.

The next week or so passes with more of the same. Our team sections rotate among the three companies, carrying out company and platoon operations, calling in fire missions of 105 artillery to support fire fights, blowing trees, evacuating three more wounded and arranging for helicopter gunships or resupply trucks that come down the one and only mine-infested road leading into the peninsula.

The road is regularly cleared of mines by a platoon of local forces from a roadside outpost, so the trucks make it through with only a few sniper rounds from the wood line. Choppers take care of that pretty quickly with bursts of suppressive fire from M60 machine guns manned by door gunners who are very happy to oblige the snipers. There is no enemy KIA that we can find. The VC snipers are good at hit and run.

This is all fairly routine for us by now. But the other day there was one especially hairy incident. Brad and I had joined Alpha Company for a three-day spell in a forward location. After a day of patrols and a few light skirmishes, the company was digging in for the night. A standard night defensive position was set up with inter-locking fields of fire reinforced by claymore mines, M60 machine guns, and predesignated targets for our 60mm mortars. We felt very safe, like masters of the jungle.

In these situations I try to stay low in a foxhole, or behind a tree or some other cover because of the unexpected sniper attacks. It is easy to be careless or to be exposed when it is necessary to move about. Unfortunately, a sniper hit an assistant machine gunner while he was lugging ammunition, but luckily he was only wounded in the shoulder and was evacuated. Even more unnerving are the number of near misses, when a round would have hit its mark if it were not for some slight movement, a turn sideways, a crouch or other life saving, split-second, lucky twist. The intended victims always have something to talk about, but forever after wonder when their number will come up.

That night, before dark, I had worked my way over to one of the flank machine gun positions with the first platoon leader. Our purpose was to inform the soldiers of preset mortar targets in front of their position. This particular position covered a likely avenue of enemy attack. It turned out to be very likely.

The lien doi lieutenant and I were crouching down in the fighting position with two soldiers looking at a map. To see the map better I removed my helmet and placed it on top of a sandbag. Just at that instant we heard the crack of a rifle. The helmet jumped off the sandbag and fell into our foxhole. There was a hole shot into one side; and the bullet had apparently spun out the bottom. We were momentarily in awe of the sniper's accuracy, and I, in particular, felt a joyous relief that the empty helmet took the bullet.

Almost immediately we heard small arms fire and the sound of whizzing bullets all around our front. We were under attack by a sizable force. Not wanting to have our heads blown off, the four of us in the foxhole raised our M16s over the front of the hole and turned on the rock and roll for Charlie. By this time others had joined in and we had a good suppressive fire to tone down Chuck's enthusiasm. When we took a look we could see a squad of VC approaching under the cover of a ditch. More enemies were firing at us from the cover of the jungle around our perimeter. It must have been at least a platoon of VC trying to penetrate our flank and overrun our defense. This was very aggressive since we probably outnumbered them, but they must have counted on the element of surprise and the fact that we were still settling in.

All of the friendlies on our side of the perimeter joined in the party. We gained enough suppressive fire that we could shoot deliberately on semiautomatic, pumping out one aimed round at a time. That slowed Chuck down. Then our mortars started peppering the area around the ditch. Just then, my M16 jammed. Some dirt must have gotten into the chamber. So I pulled out my .357 magnum and fired several well-aimed rounds. At that distance I was not having much effect, but I did wing one VC. After reloading the six-gun, I concentrated on the overall situation to see what else we could do.

The fight was over soon. The VC in the ditch retreated from our mortar fire and the Chucks in the wood line soon stopped shooting. All was still for a while. We waited, breathing quietly, ears tuned in for any sound of attack. Nothing happened.

Back at the Alpha Company command post, in the center of the perimeter, Brad and I reported in to Captain Blake at battalion headquarters. The Alpha company commander had already given Thie u ta Tan a blow-by-blow report while the fighting was going on. Our district headquarters acknowledged the report and told us to keep alert. We had no need for that advice. It was a long night of waiting for another attack that never came.

I did have a chance to practice skills in cleaning my M16 under a poncho with a red lens flashlight, the kind that prevents loss of night vision. The soiled cleaning patch showed that I had picked up some dirt, probably in the rifle barrel at the foxhole. After that I tied a rag or something else over the top of the muzzle to keep it clean.

Also this week, Doc conducted sick call for local villagers with security troops posted around. We don't care if they are friendly or VC, because we hope they will appreciate our efforts to help them and their children. Many times we just give them a bar of soap from our C-ration parcels so they can wash away the filth of the river. Other times a simple aspirin seems to work wonders. On a few occasions, Doc gives away some stronger medicine with strict instructions interpreted by Sergeant Sang. The villagers nod their heads, they smile, they seem to be genuinely appreciative of our attention, but we can't be sure they will follow Doc's guidance or if they will feel better. Some of them refer to Doc with the Vietnamese word for doctor, bac si. They say, "Bac si number one, bac si number one," as they hold up their pointer fingers. Doc smiles, and he likes the appreciative gestures, but we don't know if the same people will be shooting at us the next day.

———

My lucky day arrives. With the good wishes of the team I head out for R&R. It seems hard to believe, like I am in a protected, magical zone. A supply truck takes me out on the mine-infested road. I cannot believe that I am very close to reaching safety but only a moment away from being blown away, so I hope that mine clearing team has done its job well today. The supply chopper is a little late getting to the helipad at district, but I wait patiently with the NCO in charge of the landing procedure. The radio sounds out clear with the wobbling voice of a chopper pilot:

"Romeo One Six, Romeo One Six, this is Ishmael One One, Ishmael One One, over."

The district NCO says, "This is Romeo One Six, over."

"This is Ishmael One One, have you had enemy contact in the last two four hotels and is Lima Zulu clear? Over."

"This is Romeo One Six. No enemy contact, Lima Zulu is clear for landing. Popping smoke, over."

"This is Ishmael One One, I see yellow smoke, over."

"This is Romeo One Six, roger, yellow smoke, over."

"This is Ishmael, roger, out."

Ishmael One One comes in like he always comes in, fast and low over the treetops. Each landing is unique because you never know what might happen. The same procedure is followed. The same radio routine. All to assure that a glitch will be discovered before it becomes fatal. No pilot wants to take a bullet in the transmission or through the open doors, or anywhere else, and take a crash dive at low altitude right into the hard ground, maybe with treetops piercing your body in the swirling mess. No one on the ground wants to lose their brave resupply pilot who goes through all the chopper popping snipers, rocket shots, and bad weather to carry rations, beer, mail, ammo, and people, even a hasty medevac or fire support, all throughout the province.

It is good to hear Ishmael's voice and the sound of his chopper. The chopper sound always gives me feelings of excitement and elation. The sound of any chopper means a gunship to help in infantry tactics, or the arrival of supplies and mail, or the salvation of a medevac. The sound of Ishmael One One's voice is familiar.

He knows my call sign and I know his. He is on the radio lifeline that all grunts depend upon. He has seen me on the landing zone and I have seen him through the chopper window while giving him a thumbs up that all cargo is unloaded and he is clear for takeoff. I don't know much about his background and he doesn't know mine. We depend upon each other to survive in hostile territory. We have a bond that means a whole lot in a little bit of time, where one tick of time can be the difference between life and death.

I do not know why Ishmael One One has picked his particular call sign. When I first heard it back in Than Phu district it made me think of the novel *Moby Dick,* and the line "Call me Ishmael." Maybe he has the same adventurous spirit as that character. On second thought I recognized the deeper meaning originating in the Bible long before *Moby Dick* was written. Ishmael means wanderer, after the son of Abraham who was cast out to wander in the desert. In Hebrew it means "God listens." I think that Ishmael One One feels like a wanderer in this war and he hopes that God is listening. If God is listening to this war that keeps going on and on and consumes people in a country with a long history of war—then God is in a mighty struggle with the devil.

Ishmael sets the bird down gently. The crew chief passes out the mailbag and several ammo boxes. I give a wave to Ishmael and then push against the rush of air from the blades to hop into the open cargo bay. We are off. I feel elation to be off the ground, flying to province airfield where I will catch a flight to Saigon, and then to Hawaii for my long planned reunion with Cathy. I can hardly wait.

Thirteen

WORDS FROM HOME

Hiep and Thanh lean over a crude wooden table, pouring over a map of the Huu Dinh area. A lantern hanging off a wooden peg in an upright timber casts a warm glow and wafts the faint odor of kerosene. They are back in one of the VC hamlets in the eastern Huu Dinh.

"We have failed to stop traffic on this road," Thanh says, pointing to the road leading from the government district town. "Our sentries say that a South Vietnamese officer discovered the tank mine we placed there."

Hiep looks up and adds, "We missed the American advisors too. They were just coming down the road from the town."

Thanh sighs slightly, almost growling, "Our attack on their Alpha Company failed too."

Hiep replies, "Now we must concentrate on other areas. They are pushing us away too fast. We must do something more dramatic than mining the road and trails and starting small firefights."

"Yes," says Thanh. "Our resistance to the puppet troops is not enough. We could commit larger numbers of fighters, but that would bring the wrath of air power down on us. It would be too risky. We must do something else to discourage them, something bold."

Hiep steps a few paces to the other side of the room, turns, and says, "Maybe we should target one of their senior officers or an American advisor...but that too would incite their fury."

Thanh replies, "It may, my friend, but we can get away with it. If they come down hard on us with more aggressive tactics or artillery, then we can fade away over the river until their anger is spent. We can return when they are not on guard."

Hiep, his interest aroused, says with some enthusiasm, "If they are stunned by a bold move they may stop where they are...decide it's not worth their effort now."

Thanh adds, his voice rising to match Hiep's enthusiastic tone, "Besides, if the government troops attack us here, they will disrupt the lives and welfare of people, and that will help to rally support against the government. The people have long memories, and word of their complaints will spread to other places. That will help our overall efforts to sway the population against the government."

"Yes, my friend," says Hiep. "That is good. Let us do it."

Just then, a sentry comes to the door and says, "Good news, your friend from the north has arrived."

Their look of bewilderment turns to smiles as they see Ta Quang Thinh come through the door. They had not seen him since they left him at Cu Chi to recover from his wounds.

Thanh stands and says, "It is good to see you, my friend."

"It is good to see you too, my friends," says Thinh.

"You look well," says Hiep. "How did your wound heal?"

Thinh replies, "I received good care in the underground hospital north west of Cu Chi. The American blasts did not hurt us and good doctors from Hanoi were there. I often thought of you and longed to join your efforts near Ben Tre. I traveled on foot and then took boats through the rivers and canals to get here."

Seeing the pleased look on Hiep's face and feeling another rush of joy, Thanh says, "We are happy you are here, Thinh. It is very good to see my old friend who shares my memories of the Truong Song."

"Do you have any news?" says Hiep

"Yes I do, and a letter for Thanh, from the north, and for you Hiep, a scarf from your wife. She hopes it will be useful to you."

Hiep feels a tinge of latent sorrow overwhelmed by joy at the memory of his wife and children and the tangible expression of their love in the scarf held out by Thinh. It is square and long enough to be folded into a neckerchief, with a red and blue check pattern, the colors of the VC flag, and made of good quality cotton fabric. He thinks, my wife is so caring and practical to think of this handsome way to sooth my sweaty, hot neck in the burning sun while wearing a constant remembrance of her love.

As Hiep takes the scarf from Thinh, he says, "Thank you, my friend, for carrying my family's gift such a long way."

Thinh smiles and says, "I am happy to do it for my faithful comrade, and it is such a fine symbol of our patriotic cause. You are lucky to have such a family, my friend."

Thinh turns toward Thanh, who has seated himself, and pulls a letter from his breast pocket. It is carefully folded into a piece of protective foil from an American C-ration pack. He hands the letter to Thanh with a look of fond regard, as if he too were sharing words from home.

Looking thankfully into Thinh's eyes, Thanh nods and takes the letter. He sees it has been dated four months earlier. He knows the thoughts within could contain old news; but the loving sentiments of his father and mother could be just as comforting as the day they were written.

He decides to savor the anticipation of reading it and says, "Thinh, thank you for carrying this letter to me. I will enjoy reading it. First, tell us your news."

Thinh sits on a bamboo-sleeping platform away from the table. "Since Uncle Ho died many things have happened. His legacy is strong and the war goes well for us, especially with the growing weakness of the American government. The Americans fall apart from the inside with war protests and disagreement among their leaders. There was a very damaging story about a massacre of villagers at My Lai. American troops slaughtered innocent villagers and said they were VC. The Americans hid it for many months but the truth finally came out and now an American lieutenant is on trial. This led to even more protests against policy in

Washington. Antiwar protests have been spurred on by Nixon's attacks in Cambodia. The American people do not like his expansion of the war. One protest at a place called Kent State led to four students being killed by the National Guard soldiers."

Thanh follows Thinh's words intently, and says, "This is all good for our cause."

Thinh nods his head and continues, "Yes. The enemy is being demoralized but we still need to be wary of President Nixon because he is crafty and tough minded. But, the Americans seem to be reducing their troop strength. Our spies say it looks like more planeloads of troops are leaving than arriving in our land."

Hiep says, "Thank you for this good news, my friend. It gives me hope to renew our fight here."

Thanh adds, "Yes, it is very good news. Let us tell you about our plans."

Thanh and Hiep tell Thinh about their plans for bold action under the light of the kerosene lamp. They talk long into the night about what has happened and what they will do. They all agree that it is good plan. Thinh lets them know that he can only stay a few days to share their progress and then must go north to Tay Ninh Province where he will help plan for an offensive next year. Thinh and Hiep say they are tired and retire for the night. Thanh presses his hand against the letter in his breast pocket and decides to stay up a little longer to read it.

Thanh looks at the envelope. On the face of it, standing out from a few smudges and rain marks, his father's handwriting is still clear, in a firm hand with only slight signs of faltering from infirmity. The ink is slightly faded and is rubbed away in spots by many miles of travel in satchels over the Truong Son. The envelope is wrinkled a bit and its corners show some wear. Looking at it brings forth a welling of emotions that fills Thanh's chest and waters his eyes. He thinks it is a miracle that the letter arrived in his hands after so many miles, so many obstacles, and so much time. Now he thinks that he holds a little connection to his family here in his hands.

Thanh holds the letter lightly in the palm of his outstretched hand and bows his head as he sits hunched over, in a prayer-like position. A grateful feeling grows in him and he thinks, I am thankful for this connection to my father and mother and sister far, far away near Hanoi. Just seeing the envelope makes me feel their warmth and caring, even in this remote outpost.

With the sharp tip of an old kitchen knife he slits the envelope open and draws out the two folded sheets of paper. His father's words fill the pages:

Our dear son and brother,

Your mother, sister and I hope this will find you safe and well, wherever you are. We have not heard of you for months now, but every day we hold you in our thoughts and pray that you do not come to any harm.

We are very proud of you and the tasks you have undertaken for your homeland and all Vietnamese who want to remove invaders from our land so we can unite into one country. Our neighbors wish you to know that they have high hopes for your success in the south. We all support the efforts of our soldiers and cadre through the austerity that comes from the need to sacrifice for our war effort.

The people here continue to endure the bombs that fall on our homes and that destroy our crops, livestock, workshops, and factories. Our family is fortunate to live some distance away from Hanoi so we do not get the full effect of the American bombs, but when they come they bring much destruction. So far we

have escaped the worst in our underground shelter.

On a happy note, your sister is teaching
at the school for young children. She
enjoys this work and is doing very well
with it. Her work is her life now because
there are few social opportunities for
young people with many away in the
army. Maybe she will follow in my foot-
steps and go on to teach higher subjects
and the doctrine of Ho Chi Minh. We
will be happy if she carries on the family
tradition in education.

Your mother and I are well enough. I still
do some teaching of youths but there are
fewer of them since many volunteer to go
south as you did. Your mother and I are
busy tending our gardens and chickens,
selling a few vegetables at the market and
helping our friends get by. We are sad-
dened that our normal life is disrupted by
the war and you are so far away.

Well, dear son, we hope you keep safe
and well and come back to us soon.
Know that we are always thinking of
you and hold the spirit of our cause in

our hearts. With all our love and hope.
Father.

Thanh looks at the open pages, and feels imbued with a sense of love and purpose. After a moment he folds the letter, places it carefully back in the envelope, and puts it in his pocket. He will savor this letter every day. He touches his pocket and sighs quietly.

Fourteen

DEACON JACK

Returning from R&R in Hawaii, I am flying in another noisy cargo plane to Ben Tre airfield. Sitting in the web side-seats, my mind wanders back to the glorious week of reunion with Cathy. She flew all the way from New York with the faith and hope that I would actually show up in Honolulu. A week or more of time and events had separated our letters, so there was all the uncertainty about how fate might intervene to wreck our plans.

She picked the luxurious Kahala Hilton Hotel for our stay, saying that the military rates made it affordable and that it is worth it considering the circumstances. We rented a car to tour all over the island, especially enjoying a visit to Pearl Harbor. The memories of the earlier war somehow seemed akin to our nation's current struggles on the Pacific Rim.

I was sad to miss seeing our baby daughter who was with her grandparents back home. But, it didn't seem

right to bring a baby half way around the world with all
the uncertainties of our situation. Also, I am not sure I
could stand the pain of parting with my only child again
while facing the gulf of time and events that awaited me
back in Vietnam.

Along with the luxury of the hotel, the beauty of the
beaches, the lights of Waikiki, and the majesty of the
hills, there was sheer joy in being together to share precious moments. It was a respite from difficulties like the
tension of separation, not knowing how the other is at
any given moment, the fears conjured up by imagination
after shocking newscasts about death and destruction
in Vietnam. It was a temporary break from the feeling
of helplessness that comes with knowing it is impossible to help a loved one who may be in need. To me, the
memory of R&R is like an oasis of tranquility and happiness amid the dangers and disruptions of my reality.

As the plane descends toward the airfield I think
that it won't be long until I am back with my team. It will
just take the time to report in to headquarters, maybe
catch a truck ride or a hop with Ishmael 11 to the district
town, and then go out to the team by jeep on that nasty
road in the Huu Dinh. When its roaring engines halt the
plane I wonder what has happened while I was gone.

The back ramp of the cargo plane comes down and
Sergeant First Class Fowler, the NCO in charge of the airfield, arrives in a three-quarter-ton truck to pick up boxes

of ammo, beer, cartons of c-rations, and assorted gear. Specialist Chovinowski is still riding shotgun and gives me a nod of recognition with a faint smile on his face.

Sergeant Fowler says, "Hello Lieutenant. How was your R&R?"

"Oh, great. We had a good time in Hawaii. Anything big happen here?"

He pauses a moment, with a pained look on his face, and says, "Yeah. You know Ishmael One One?"

I look at him with concern and say, "Yeah?"

"Well, I'm sorry to say he went down three days ago. Hit the ground hard. His chopper is in pieces. It didn't autogyrate down to a soft landing. They say he took rounds in the gearbox. His transmission locked up. Charlie is always shooting at our birds. He was a great guy."

I just look at him as a dark cloud of emotion presses down on me, starting with my head, and leaving me with a heavy heart and numb legs.

After a moment I say, "Aghh, that's terrible. I liked him, didn't know him that well, because I always saw him in his whirlybird. He covered me in a fire fight, gave me a ride last week to R&R."

"Sorry to give you the news. Bad stuff happens fast around here. Everybody is down about it. He was a regular part of the operation, nice guy, always making chopper runs when you needed him."

Sergeant Fowler shakes off the heavy feelings and says, "The only other things that happened were two more rocket attacks on the Vietnamese headquarters in Ben Tre. The brass is hopping mad about it. Your Charlies in the Huu Dinh didn't go on vacation while you were gone. You're probably gonna get a pep talk about dealin' with 'em."

"Yeah," I say, "a grunt's work is never done."

After loading the supplies, we get in the truck and head to Ben Tre.

—

Later that day I arrive at our Vietnamese battalion headquarters, still the same spot in the Huu Dinh. Brad greets me with all the usual questions about my trip to Hawaii, but does allow that he liked his R&R in Australia.

"Hawaii is good for married guys but for single guys Australia is much better. You can meet all those nice round-eye women," he says.

"Yeah, I know you like to party with those Aussie Sheilas," I reply.

"That's where I'm going next time. Won't be long now," Brad says.

"Good plan, Brad. How about what's going on here?"

He says, "Captain Blake, Clarkee, Sang, and Doc went with Alpha Company. They're forward on our right flank. We'll go with Bravo Company on the forward left flank when they get back."

"OK. Anything special going on?" I ask. "We need to do something different. I got an earful from the colonel about needing to make more progress."

"Yeah. We're talking more with the locals, trying to reassure them everything will be better after we push the VC out of the area. Other than that, it's routine patrols, with a few brief enemy contacts."

I reply, "Maybe the talk will help."

"Don't know about progress," Brad says. "We think blowing down trees is progress, but some of the villagers spoke up about it and they don't seem happy. I think they are still helping Charlie."

"What do you mean?" I ask.

"Right near the fort here, one of our guys hit a trip wire and set off a bunch of those mackerel can grenades. Some VC must've snuck back around our forward companies to hit us. If the locals are on our side they might've reported it."

"Yeah," I say. "No place is safe. We need to do more, maybe get Doc to do more sick calls for the villagers. Maybe just blow trees with VC flags."

Brad nods and says, "That sounds good to me...Oh yeah, tomorrow our headquarters group is going forward to Alpha Company to get a more detailed report from the company commander."

"That'll be good," I say in a hopeful tone.

———

The next day is clear and bright. The sky is blue with no rain in sight and the warming air is only moderately humid. We walk up the trail toward Alpha Company. Thieu u ta Tan is in the middle of the column. Ahead of him on point is a squad from Charlie Company, the reserve. Brad and I follow behind the major and his staff officers. Another squad of riflemen is behind us. We stay somewhat spread out in case of attack, but we are fairly confident that we will not run into too much since

Alpha company has been all over the area in the past few days. I think that it would be unlikely to run into more than an enemy squad and we have enough firepower to deal with that. In the event that a larger enemy force has skirted our forward companies to attack us, we can always hunker down and call for reinforcements.

As the sun rises the cool of the morning fades away and is replaced by a warmer, humid air that makes us sweat. Perspiration gathers on the sweatband of my helmet and soaks the neckerchiefs that we wear to absorb the wet. The jungle canopy provides some shade and I think that this is a lot better than being out in an exposed rice paddy, slopping through the mud with the hot sun beating right down and knocking the tar out of you.

Thie u ta Tan talks on his field radio, keeping touch with Alpha and Bravo companies. The tall, thin XO, as the executive officer is known, Dai uy Quan, who speaks good English, interprets for me, saying that he is pleased the companies have advanced with no serious casualties and with only limited sniper fire to slow them. He says that we may be able to establish a new headquarters farther into the Huu Dinh. Meanwhile, we hear the blasts of dynamite from trees being blown down in the new territory.

We arrive at a place where trails cross and make a small open space. There is a thatched hut to the right side with a porch and tables. It is a sort of tavern or teahouse where people can get a coke or tea or even a chunk of ice brought in by boat. The front porch, shaded with palm fronds, looks welcoming in the heat of the day. Thie u ta Tan puts up his hand to call a halt to the column. Men spread out into the surrounding jungle to set up a secure perimeter.

Thie u ta Tan steps onto the porch of the store and peers inside. When the proprietor steps out of the door with a towel in hand the Major asks for a pot of tea. As the proprietor nods his head in affirmation the Major waves his hand for the other officers to join him. I think it is amazing that hot tea feels good even on a hot day.

Just as I am stepping on to the porch there is a commotion around the back of the store.

One of our riflemen comes running around the building yelling, "VC, VC, VC running away. Detonator! It's a trap."

His platoon leader rushes over as the man gestures behind the store. Hearing all of this, Brad and I have our weapons at port arms and are heading around the building. We find that about thirty feet behind the store, behind a thicket of jungle bush, there is an electric detonator lying on the ground near a set of footprints. It is the kind you squeeze to create a current and spark off a blasting cap that ignites larger explosives.

After some discussion among the Vietnamese soldiers Dai uy Quan explains that the rifleman had gone behind the store to relieve himself. He saw someone running away down the trail. He shouted for the intruder to halt but it was too late. He had disappeared. After getting his buddy to cover the trail, the rifleman found footprints coming from the spot where the detonator lay.

Further investigation shows us that the detonator is attached to two black wires that lead off on an angle into the brush behind the store and toward the trail in the direction of our travel. By this time several of our men had gone down the trail about one hundred paces beyond the store, and found a large mine. It is dozens of times larger than the mackerel can booby traps that we usually encounter. It is circular, almost a foot across and several inches thick. It contains enough explosives to blow up a tank. The two black wires are attached to it so that it could be command detonated by the man who ran away. There is little doubt that it had been intended to blow away our headquarters group.

Our point squad had not seen the mine. They were allowed to walk by so that bigger prey could be killed. If Major Tan had not stopped for a cup of tea many of us would have been dead by now. It would have been a big explosion, big enough to blow away a chunk of the jungle and every one within the considerable blast area. It would have been so fierce that those of us in front of it would have been shredded and those ahead and behind would have thousands of pieces of shrapnel whip into their flesh and tear their bodies apart. Some might be knocked down by the blast and have only surface wounds, it would have taken a large toll and wiped out the headquarters group.

"It gives me the creeps, Brad," I say. "If we hadn't stopped for a break, that VC would have taken out the battalion command group, including the Major, the XO, and a bunch of others, even with us spread out."

Brad grunts a "Yeah."

Staring down at the disarmed mine, Brad says, "Holy kamoli, look at that bad boy. That could ruin your whole day!"

I say, "That Charlie was just standing behind the bush waiting for us to approach. Probably got word from the locals that we were heading this way. He must have been surprised when we stopped. It ruined his plan for sure."

After a few more minutes of chatter and awed appreciation for the fates that saved us from catastrophe, we fall back into the habitual nonchalance and thick-skinned posture of typical field grunts. Thie u ta Tan signals for his group to continue moving down the trail. Soldiers adjust their web gear and check their M16s.

Brad says, "It don't mean nothing."

"All in a day's work." I reply.

But we all know we beat the odds by a hair, lucked out over the cunning of Charlie who definitely wanted us dead.

We go down the trail again. After a few minutes Thie u ta Tan halts the movement. We find out from Captain Quan that the Major has changed his mind about a rendezvous with Alpha Company today. After the big mine incident he decides to return to our headquarters fort in the big clearing to direct a new operation. He wants to be sure we chase out any more pockets of VC that are operating behind the forward companies. We don't know if the mine ambush involved just one VC or if there are squads of them that have circled around us. Charlie Company is ordered to have two platoons sweep the area again, with a third platoon in reserve back at the fort.

I call Captain Blake on the field radio. "Roughneck Six, Roughneck Six, This is Roughneck Three Five."

He responds, "Roughneck Three Five, This is Six, over."

"This is Three Five, we report contact with enemy saboteur trying to command detonate bomb on our trail. Enemy escaped. No casualties, over."

"This is Six, roger. Good work. Glad you are OK. We are getting word now from our counterparts."

"This is Three Five, we are returning to previous Charlie Papa [command post]. Elements of Charlie Company sweeping area. Over."

"This is Six, roger. We will be with Alpha in November Delta Papa [night defensive position]. We had two sniper contacts in the last four hotels [hours]. No casualties. Any further? Over."

"This is Three Five, negative further. Keep your eyes open. Out."

I can picture John Blake standing by the field radio, the long spiral cord of the handset reaching to his ear. The two highly polished handles of his twin .45 caliber pistols protruding from their custom holsters, one on each side. Then I imagine a VC attack where he draws both pistols and blazes away with deadly accuracy. It would be quite a sight indeed. In my imagined scene, Mr. Charles cannot swing and level an AK-47 as fast as Blake can aim and fire. In close combat Blake has the advantage and is the victor. Then I think, "How much have cowboy movies clouded my appreciation of good army training?"

Our command group returns to the headquarters fort secured by the third platoon of Charlie Company.

We monitor radio reports from the company's first and second platoons. They are each spread out in "wedge" formations, slowly moving through our supposedly captured areas, checking for VC activity, looking for concealed underground fighting positions, ammunition caches, booby traps, and, of course, VC fighters. The wedge formations are useful when the enemy's location is unknown, because our men can move quickly but respond easily to enemy contact on the point.

The afternoon wears on. There is one report of an enemy cache of mackerel can explosives. Apparently, Charles had assembled the supplies to manufacture booby traps in a small clearing, and then hid two dozen in a hole lightly covered with palm fronds. They must have had plans to continue making them because not all of the supplies had been turned into lethal devices. There is no doubt that the grenades would soon be put to use against our troops. Our movements must have interrupted their plans to deploy their traps.

The sun is getting low in the sky. Thie u ta Tan calls the Charlie Company platoons into the battalion command post for the night. We will establish our night perimeter and resume searching tomorrow. After we are sure the area is clear, we will dynamite down more trees for better visibility, giving special priority to those with the painted VC flags.

Meanwhile Alpha and Bravo companies will hold their positions with a defensive perimeter and send out squad-sized patrols to scout enemy activity. Brad and I settle down to a meal of rice topped with pork slices from a small C-ration can.

———

After another night in the hammock, I awake to the chill, damp air as a bright sun rises. We rely on our fatigues to keep us warm since we have left ponchos and quilted liners back at base to make more room in our small TA-50 packs for canned food. When it comes to luxury, food tops warmth as long as it is mostly warm through the night. To me, a can of chili is better than a chopped duck.

Brad must have had bad dreams. At one point during the night he half awoke me with mumbled words. It was as if he were encouraging soldiers during a firefight. He talked through the attack in his dreams and fidgeted in his hammock before quieting down. I guess the specter of being blown away by the big mine yesterday unsettled him a bit.

I decide to shave off two days growth so I can greet the day like a civilized person. The razor is a luxury that takes up almost no space and it is a way to feel a little cleaner when there are no showers or baths for days on end. There is a rain barrel in the fort where it is convenient to fill my steel pot with some water. Using a small bar of soap I make lather and pull out my razor. It is a rough shave without hot water and good shaving cream. The blade is dull from repeated use and being banged about in my pack. Without a mirror I try to place the sharp steel on my face by touch and feel with the hope I am gong in the best direction for the terrain over my cheeks and chin. What a luxury a mirror would be.

Just as I am finishing up I hear an exclamation in the direction of the radiotelephone operator. He gives the hand set to Thie u ta Tan and waves me over.

"Dai uy Blake bi thuong!" exclaims the Major with a shocked look.

He puts down the handset and speaks to Dai uy Quan in a rush of words.

The Vietnamese word for "wounded" fills my head as the Major looks in my eyes with a disbelief that matches mine.

My pulse quickens and my senses go on full alert. Brad walks over from his hammock and looks at me with a question in his eyes.

"Captain Blake is wounded?"

Dai uy Quan says, "Captain Blake has been shot by a sniper. He stood up outside the command post. The sniper hit him with a single round. Captain Blake is bleeding but Bac si Jackson is treating him. The Alpha Company commander has a squad ready to carry him to a clearing."

Brad grabs our radio and calls district headquarters for a medevac. As he says the word "urgent," I hear the Major's radio operator. Another voice is coming through his handset.

It is the Alpha Company commander. I make out the words "Dai uy Blake chet." I know the Vietnamese words for "death." Thie u ta Tan and Dai uy Quan look at me with mournful concern. It is not just a blow to our team to lose a member; it is a blow to them to lose an ally under their protection. I look at Brad and he looks at me. We see the shock and loss in each other's eyes. Our expressions say another good man has been brought down. Family and friends will feel the pain.

———

Sergeant Clarkson, Doc, and Trung si Sang all go in the chopper with Captain Blake's body out to province airfield. We are all called back to province headquarters. The people there all know about the sniper attack. Such news travels fast. They express their condolences to us as they see our team members around the compound.

People are in the habit of containing their shock and sorrow. Death has been a regular visitor to our province and there is little time for extended grieving. Rather, sentiments are shared with the common understanding among soldiers that we are all facing imminent mortality. Anyone can be next. Even the men in support and supply jobs could be hit by a rocket, a sniper's bullet, or a booby trap. There is always the possibility of another Tet attack like the one that left countless bullet holes in the walls of the government buildings in Ben Tre.

Blake's death took big chunks out of each one of us on MAT 23. He was one of us. He took shared memories with him. We had helped each other through rough patches. He knew our stories and we knew his. We miss his friendly, thoughtful ways. We have lost a brother in arms.

There is a brief funeral for Captain Blake in the province compound. The ceremony follows protocol. His M16 with bayonet is thrust into the ground, boots placed in front, helmet on top of the butt. Even his signature custom .45 caliber pistols are placed neatly in the display. We slowly file past, turn with precision, and salute in his honor. Everyone there is grim and respectful. We all move slowly and deliberately through the ceremony so we can prolong parting with a cherished friend.

Afterward, we sit in the shade of the pavilion under the fading sun of the afternoon recalling good memories and giving tributes to Blake, all presided over by our newly named deacon, Jack Dickens. As the bottle of Jack Dickens Black Label Kentucky Straight Bourbon Whiskey is passed around, each of us raises it up and gives a tribute to Captain Blake before taking a swig.

"Here's to John Blake."

"Here's to a good man."

"A brave man, a good soldier."

"Hail Blake, brave centurion"

"To Captain Blake."

"May he rest in peace with honor."

Around and around it goes. The Jack Dickens dulls our pain with each draught.

When the pace of tributes slows, Clarkee says, "I hate to see another good man sent to Dover."

We all know that the dead from Nam go to the Dover Air Force Base for processing by the mortuary unit. I picture a large cargo plane filled with row after row of silver colored, metallic caskets, each draped with the Stars and Stripes.

Doc says, "I wonder if Blake's former wife will pay her respects?" He passes the bottle of Jack Black over to Brad.

Brad puts his hand around the almost empty bottle of bourbon and pauses, saying, "Will she be haunted for life after writing that "Dear John" letter?"

"Dunno about her," I say, "but imagine the grief of his parents. They know he died before all the protest songs, peace marches, Paris negotiations, or the Big Green Army Machine could end the war."

Clarkee coughs lightly after taking a swig, and says, "Ya know, Captain Blake's father sent him those beautiful, polished .45s. He was the best shot around. Shooting them was a bond they both loved. But even all that didn't save 'im."

"Yeah," I say, "it was almost like nothing could happen to him...I guess luck doesn't come that easy."

As we talk around the table, every man there from our team, and others too, express the belief that as deep as a father's grief may be, there is no pain greater than a mother's when she loses her child. As Deacon Jack Dickens encourages words from the mourners, every man allows that they would never want to put their mother through that kind of pain. Somehow Deacon Jack brings out the idea that if it were up to mothers then children would not go off to war. Any miscreant who even talked about war as a way of solving problems would be dealt with sternly before things could get out of hand.

Deacon Jack makes his rounds. The conversation tapers off. The sun is going down. Another bottle gets passed around the table.

> The deacon went down
> To the cellar to pray,
> But he got drunk
> And he stayed all day.
>
> He drank and he drank
> And mourned all the men,
> The ones he knew
> He wouldn't see again.

Fifteen

THE ELEPHANT

Thanh and Hiep are talking to the sniper who killed Captain Blake. They sit under a tree in the center of a small Hamlet controlled by their VC forces.

Hiep says, "You have done well, Tran Luc."

Tran Luc smiles faintly, with a knowing look in his eyes as he slowly nods his head twice. He is a middle-aged man, a carpenter with a wife and three children. Tran Luc is angry with the actions of the government and the heavy-handed, corrupt ways of officials. He fears being pushed from his home. The government pushed his parents from their home in the upper Huu Dinh to a so-called strategic hamlet. He wants to do what ever he can to stop the American war and be rid of the puppet government. A modest, hardworking family man, Tran Luc takes no pleasure in killing with his highly regarded skill as a marksman.

As one of the best VC snipers, Tran Luc's latest mission was to kill a ranking member of the government's Alpha Company. A VC reconnaissance team had found the precise location of Alpha Company. It was also know that the American captain was with them.

Tran Luc's assignment was part of the overall plan to strike hard at the invaders. One team would ambush the battalion command group, and the other team would support Tran Luc in a high profile sniper attack. By the time it moved out, the sniper team already knew the attempt to blow away the battalion command group had failed when an unexpected turn of events thwarted a command detonated blast. They felt that they needed to do something dramatic.

Hiep remembers Tran Luc's modest ways and his reputation for not being a braggart as he softly says, "Tell us how you accomplished your mission, Tran Luc."

Tran Luc pauses, his face showing no emotion, and gives a slight shrug as he begins to relate what happened. Thanh and Hiep listen intently.

At the first light of dawn, Tran Luc had gone with a squad of VC fighters to a spot about a half-kilometer away from the Alpha Company perimeter. The squad stayed to wait for him at this position to divert any government patrols and to assist Tran Luc if he encountered difficulties. He proceeded alone because he planned to rely on a slow, quiet, stealthy approach to the enemy position where he could wait quietly for a target of opportunity.

Tran Luc started his approach toward Alpha Company by walking, at first quickly, then more slowly. The jungle canopy had not been destroyed by government troops and the underbrush provided good cover. He pushed deliberately through the thick growth, stopping frequently to listen for sounds of troop movements. As he drew near to the enemy perimeter he crouched in the shadows to observe any enemy activity or listening posts. He patiently waited, listened, and looked before moving on. Finally, he crawled on his belly, pushing with his legs and elbows, the rifle cradled in his arms.

The enemy had cleared brush away from their perimeter to make a clear field of fire for their weapons. They had done their job well. There was little brush around the perimeter and the trees thinned out toward the jungle growth. Tran Luc figured he could get a good shot from the protection of the surrounding jungle.

He took up a position in the shadows, well concealed by thick vegetation. He laid there, his sniper rifle resting lightly on his left arm with the butt angling back toward his right side in a ready position. A round was already locked and loaded in the chamber ready to fire. He was proud to have been trusted with the rifle. It was a Japanese bolt-action sniper rifle captured during their invasion of Vietnam during World War II. Because he cared for the tools of his trade, he had learned even more about the rifle. It was a Type 97 with a 2.5 power scope that fired a 6.5mm round. The four intertwined cannon balls engraved on its receiver were the mark of the Kokura Arsenal where it was manufactured. It also bore the symbol of the Japanese emperor, the flower pattern of a chrysanthemum. He was thankful that the rifle was known to show little flash and smoke due to its long barrel, a significant advantage for a sniper trying to avoid detection. Tran Luc thought that the rifle was older than he and most of the other combatants in this area.

Tran Luc liked the idea of fighting with the sniper rifle. It was a deliberate, exacting, process that required ancient skills and patience to be stealthy and purposeful, like the carpentry he so much enjoyed. He had to control his body and mind to focus on a target and carefully pull the trigger. This is much different from the aggressive movements and frantic automatic fire that most of the fighters employed. He did not enjoy the wild killing of the war and preferred, if he had to kill his enemy, to do it with the poise of a marksman and with regard for each life he must take.

The sun rose in the sky and the morning damp began to burn off. Tran Luc watched for signs of enemy activity. The soldiers mostly lay in their fighting positions, well dug into the jungle floor with cut tree branches and dirt piled around them. They occasionally moved about to communicate or relieve themselves. Tran Luc wanted better targets than the rank-and-file troops.

He saw some activity in the center of the perimeter near a well-reinforced fighting position. A cluster of radio antennas in the position suggested it was where the command group had dug in. A tall man, larger than most Vietnamese, in an American uniform, walked from the command post to a forward position. It was the American advisor. He had pistols strapped to his sides and this was known to be the American captain. The American ducked into the forward fighting position, perhaps to check the soldiers there.

Tran Luc thought that he would shoot when the American emerged from the protected position. He slowly moved his rifle into a good shooting stance, sling pulling tightly against his left arm to steady his aim. It would be a clean, easy shot. He anticipated he would make the shot, then wriggle backward and roll down a slight depression in the terrain. The government troops would not detect his movement and would not know where the shot came from. He would then crouch and walk calmly away from the area. He would be gone in the few moments it would take the government troops to recover from the shock. There would be a pause, a moment of confusion, and then the government troops would spray the wood line on full automatic fire from their M16s and M60 machine guns. By that time they would be shooting at a phantom.

Tran Luc waited maybe ten minutes holding the rifle lightly. The American emerged from the fighting position. He stepped behind a tree, apparently stretching his torso. Tran Luc anticipated the Captain's next step. He aimed. His target stepped out from behind the tree. He smoothly squeezed the trigger and the rifle spit out its deadly round with a crack. The Captain spun and went down in an instant.

Thanh and Hiep listen to every detail of Tran Luc's story, nodding their heads in encouragement.

Hiep says, "You are a brave patriot, Tran Luc. I admire your courage and skill. Your actions will help protect our homeland."

Tran Luc averts his eyes downward and quietly says, "Cam on," meaning thank you.

He is pleased that he has done what he must do, but he is not overjoyed. He would rather be left to do his carpentry and care for his family.

Thanh says, "Hiep, now we must put out a warning to our forces. We have angered the enemy and they will come after us with a vengeance."

"You are right, we must act quickly."

Thanh signals to a platoon leader that he wants to talk to. He explains that it is important to send runners and use available radios to let all VC fighters and villagers know the enemy has been hit hard and to expect reprisals. He instructs all fighters to withdraw to safe areas, across the river if necessary, to let the anger of the enemy play out. Only a few fighters are to remain to offer resistance. They are to take no risks until they have new instructions to gather for the next initiative. The platoon leader nods and says that all will be done.

——

Later that day Thanh and Hiep are drinking from glass cups of tea, seated at a small wooden table with the pot between them, sheltered from the afternoon sun under the porch roof of a palm-thatched house. They are in a hamlet further out on the peninsula, a few kilometers from the government forces. Lookouts are posted along trails leading to the hamlet. They feel safe. In the distance they can see three helicopters circling the area of the government troops like angry hornets, no doubt searching for them.

Hiep says, "Thanh, we have the puppet forces off balance. It is a great insult to the battalion commander to have one of his advisors killed. He may be recalled for a reprimand or relieved of command. They have all lost face with the Americans. Maybe they will withdraw for a while."

"Yes," says Thanh, "or maybe they will strengthen their efforts here. They may be demoralized whatever they do. Perhaps we should strike another blow before they can make any big moves."

Hiep says, "Yes, my friend, perhaps we should press them further. Any ideas?"

Thanh gazes up at the treetops, then leans forward on his stool and says, "I recall lessons from the Chinese warrior and philosopher Sun Tzu. He is the one who said we must use knowledge to win. Use deception. Confuse and divide the enemy. Attack when we have the advantage."

Hiep leans back slightly, and says, "That is good, but isn't that a higher level strategy?"

"Ahh yes," says Thanh, smiling slightly, "but the same principles work here. We do well when we confuse the enemy, disrupt their plans, and only attack when it is right for us. We get them to expend their energies, resources, and manpower to chase us. The enemy will soon be too exhausted to fight or realize that it is useless to fight us."

Hiep reflects a moment and says, "I think that we have tried to do that, but they have large numbers of soldiers, helicopters, artillery, and all types of weapons and firepower. They are strong and powerful. How can we prevail against such force, especially when they are angry?"

"My friend," says Thanh, with conviction, "we will prevail because we will use their own anger to defeat them. They will strike on impulse, waste their strength, and act without gain. We will move like the shadow they cannot catch, and they will wear themselves out. It is the teaching of Sun Tzu. We are doing it here in our own area, and it works for the whole country."

Thanh continues, "Our enemy in America does not heed the advise of Sun Tzu. They are weak in the things they should measure. When they are weak and confused at the highest levels of leadership it causes weakness all the way through their lowest ranks. This helps us defeat our adversaries right here. Their aim is not the aim of most people in this country."

Hiep says, "That is true."

Thanh replies, "If we follow ancient wisdom and we are lucky we can take advantage of enemy weakness. The big elephant will get sick and fall before it tramples us."

Hiep, nodding his head slowly, says, "I like to hear you talk of the sick elephant, but I am not sure that the elephant in the Huu Dinh is too sick. This enemy has done well. They have avoided many of our traps and our gains have been hard won."

Thanh replies, "You are right, my friend, we cannot be sure yet. This is not the usual Saigon elephant. Perhaps they too follow the wisdom of Sun Tzu. There are risks. Things do not always go well for us. Let us test the elephant further."

Hiep asks, "What do you have in mind to do that?"

"We must do something that will surprise them, provoke them, and further their confusion from the death of the American captain," says Thanh.

Hiep replies, "Perhaps we should kill the American lieutenant? That will take out all of the advisor officers."

"Yes," says Thanh, "that would push them further, but I think that for now we should try something different so they do not think we have only one trick in our pack."

"Perhaps we should make a surprise attack behind their forward units," says Hiep.

"That is a very good idea!" says Thanh, eyes wide and voice rising with enthusiasm.

The two VC leaders talk more about their surprise attack. They decide that when the enemy settles down in a few days they will move several squads of fighters to a hamlet near the headquarters of the puppet soldiers. Stealth will be required to move around the forward enemy units. These squads will let the villagers know that the VC still rule the area. Unwary enemy patrols will be ambushed or attacked to inflict maximum casualties and confusion. It will show the people of the hamlet that the puppet soldiers do not control the area. The enemy soldiers will be demoralized when they realize their tactics only work for a short time. The big problem is how to escape after the VC fighters create a disturbance in the hamlet.

They come up with a time-honored solution. After visiting the hamlet, they will initially hole up in a series of underground hideouts and spider holes already in the area; and then when the puppet forces move in to investigate the disturbance, let them pass and escape to safety. When the enemy is tricked and confused, VC fighters will return again to ambush, attack and further upset the enemy plans. Hiep and Thanh are pleased with themselves; it is such a very clever plan. The enemy will tire of fighting the phantom of the Huu Dinh.

Sixteen

DEEP WATER

After Captain Blake's funeral we return to the lien doi headquarters at the same place where we had left it in the Huu Dinh. Thie u ta Tan greets us at the fort gate saying, "I am glad you have returned."

"Thank you, sir," I say.

He warmly shakes hands with me, Doc, Brad, Clarkee, and Sang saying, "We deeply feel the loss of Captain Blake. I liked Captain Blake and thought he was a very dedicated advisor. He was a brave and efficient officer. I believe we our lucky to have your entire team working with us too. When you are ready, we will brief you on our operations."

I say, "Cam on, Thie u ta Tan. We miss Captain Blake, but we are ready to work with you. We will be ready to talk of plans as soon as we drop our gear."

As we enter the fort, the soldiers wave respectfully, or nod their heads in a sign of affirmation. Dai uy Quan walks over to greet us and express his sympathies, as do each of the staff officers and unit commanders from Charlie Company. I feel a renewed bond with them in the depth of our shared losses—Captain Blake and the killed and wounded men of our battalion.

During our brief absence the battalion has been conducting multiple sweeping operations, trying to root out VC fighters. But the VC seemingly have vanished and there have been no enemy contacts. At the same time, officials from the district town have visited the local hamlets in an effort to gain the support of the people.

I recall my meeting with the colonel and his staff back at the province headquarters. They think we need to make more progress in the Huu Dinh and that Captain Blake's death requires more persistent efforts to deal with the VC and pacify the area. I was instructed to resume advisory operations and also informed that a new captain would eventually arrive to join the team.

For now it is me, Sergeant First Class Bradford, Sergeant First Class Clarkson, Doc Jackson, and Trung si Sang. I plan to try to improve our intelligence gathering on the nature, size, and activities of the enemy while also increasing the frequency of medical visits to the hamlets. We will deploy our MAT as before, usually dividing into two teams, rotating between the companies, with one team occasionally going back to province for administration, rest, and resupply.

After a few days with the battalion, we initiate another full team effort to run a medical clinic for the hamlets near the fort. A security perimeter of riflemen is put in place around the clinic site to prevent VC intrusion. Doc sets up a table under a coconut tree in a wide spot near several thatched houses. A few crates serve as seats. Several parents line up with small children to await whatever care Doc can provide. While Brad and Clarkee keep an eye on security, Sang and I assist Doc. We have some training in first aid, but mostly we hand out soap to the parents and candy to the kids.

The villagers come from all around. No doubt many of them have VC sentiments, but as before, we are happy to help them.

I smile at Sang and say, "Maybe this is the way we can win over the population. Maybe they won't want to fight if they see us as friends"

He smiles slightly and says, "Do you think this will win some hearts and minds, LT?

"Maybe, if it doesn't get contaminated by bad actions from district or province government."

Sang gives me a knowing look and says, "Yes...too many forced relocations of farmers, too much corruption by officials, too many civilians killed by artillery."

"Yeah," I reply while thinking, "No wonder the VC can claim to offer a better life for the average Vietnamese."

During a pause in the activity I walk over to Brad, who is watching over riflemen on the edge of the hamlet and say, "Maybe today's aid will give us a day of grace but I wouldn't let my guard down."

He nods as he exhales smoke from a Lucky Strike.

———

The next day an old man, a local villager I recognize from the medical clinic, comes to our headquarters. He tells Dai uy Quan that he has seen a large gathering of perhaps twenty-five or thirty VC on the other side of the hamlet we had just visited, only about two clicks away. The VC are making their presence known and telling villagers they will receive better support from the National Liberation Front if only the government can be overthrown. Even more disturbing is the location of the VC behind Bravo Company's position. I think our medical clinic efforts have paid off with the loyalty of the old man but still wonder if this is a trap.

We huddle with Thie u ta Tan and Dai uy Quan. We are confident there are not enough VC in the area to overwhelm us, but we do not know if the VC plan to attack the rear of Bravo Company or possibly our own headquarters position. We think it is unlikely that they just want to parade through the hamlets. We decide to set our own trap.

With Charlie Company attached to headquarters as reserve in our location, and Bravo on the other side of the VC position, we can reposition elements of Alpha Company on the right so the VC are flanked on all sides except near the river. We plan to attack from the river with two platoons from Charlie Company reinforced with machine gun elements from Charlie Company's weapons platoon, if we can muster a landing craft. That will drive the VC into one of more of the other positions set up as blocking forces to snare them.

We rule out the use of artillery to avoid hurting any villagers. Better to show the locals that we can out-fight and out-maneuver the VC. Meanwhile, we request helicopter gunships to standby in case backup is needed, especially since only one rifle platoon and the heavy weapons platoon of Charlie company will be the blocking force near headquarters. We reason that they can prevail against this enemy force since they are dug in and have a reasonably secure area to their rear. Plus, Alpha company can send reinforcements if needed.

Brad and I plan to go with the two Charlie Company platoons that comprise the river assault force, about sixty men in all. The big landing craft comes plowing down the river and right up to the muddy edge where it lowers its heavy, wide ramp door. It looks like an old WWII navy boat and belches smoke from its powerful diesel engines. The door is ten to fifteen feet wide. I don't really get a chance to get a more careful look because we are all sloshing through mud and water trying to step up onto the ramp. Although we are organized and orderly in our efforts, there is a lot of noise from the rattle of rifles, bandoliers, grenades, M72 LAW antitank rocket launchers, and several M60 machine guns.

We pack in against the steel walls of the landing craft but there is still room so NCOs can move around and organize men for the assault. The big engines smoke and roar, the boat slides off the bank, and we are off to our rendezvous with the nasty side of fate. Brad and I stand stoically in the middle of the pack off to the starboard side. We did not plan to be in this particular spot since we just shuffled in with the rest, but I think it is a good location if the open door of the landing craft is greeted with a hail of AK-47 rounds. A few of the troops look at us, probably wondering how much we are sweating it. They look to see if we have our radio antenna up. To me their looks convey the request that we should be ready to call in more firepower if things get tough. Maybe their looks don't mean it, but that is what is going through my mind.

The landing craft makes its ponderous way down the river. The Vietnamese soldiers talk quietly among themselves so only an occasional soft, nervous laugh can be heard. The soldiers seem alert and ready for the fight, but without visible enthusiasm, as if it is just another part of their working day. That is mostly accurate except that it is not the usual thing for an infantryman to be packed in a can and pushed out the open end without any dirt to dive into when the bullets come flying.

I try to imagine the opening moments of our attack. The worst case is the VC firing intensely at our opening door. I am doing the combat math in my head. If there are twenty VC with AK-47s and they each fire a twenty-round clip at full automatic right at the door opening of this tub, then that's four hundred rounds coming in within the first few seconds. If they have thirty-round magazines, then that's six hundred rounds. If the first few guys soak up the lead, then the rest of us have a few seconds before Charlie can lock and load another magazine. If there are thirty VC then that's more math, and more bullets.

To deal with this our machine gunners on top of the landing craft will have to pour on enough suppressive fire to keep enemy heads down until our guys get off the ramp, hit the ground, and start pumping out waves of bullets. Once we get the VC to keep their heads down, we can shoot and move to advance against them. One unit lays down a base of fire and the other runs toward the enemy while the enemy is supposedly ducking a hail of bullets. It's like a gunfight in the old western movies where one guy says to his partner, "Cover me," and then makes a dash for it.

Now I remember that we forgot to tell the NCOs to get some guys out there fast to lay down a base of suppressive fire so the VC keep their heads down while we offload this beast. Then I come to my senses and realize that these NCOs and privates are experienced in combat and nobody needs to tell them anything about how and when to shoot back and maneuver against the enemy.

We are counting on the element of surprise, a better than two-to-one attack ratio, we hope, and standby gunships to overwhelm Mr. Charles. If we are lucky the VC expect us to attack from the forest where they would have set up booby traps and concentrated their efforts on defense. If our plan of attack from the river is successful then they might be surprised and disoriented and put up a weak resistance. Once they feel the force of our attack they might defend only a short while and then try to vanish into the jungle. Then our blocking forces will come into play.

Brad says, "LT, this looks like one of those World War II movies. This boat is a big target. It kind of makes you pucker up, doesn't it?"

"Yeah Brad...keep it tight and you'll be all right," I say, in only a half joking tone.

At the same time I feel a little weak in the knees as the adrenaline starts to flow. Now I just want to move, to make a reckless commitment to eternity.

Brad replies, "This ain't exactly as bad as the Rangers had it at Pointe Du Hoc! But if a bullet catches you it means the same thing!"

"What happened at Point Du Hoc, Brad?"

"That's where the Second Ranger Battalion climbed the hundred-foot cliffs of Normandy on D-Day with the Germans on top shooting down and throwing grenades at them. They landed on the beach in craft like this. Its one of my favorite pieces of history."

"Yeah," I say, "this is a cakewalk compared to that. Just the same, stick close so we can cover each other."

The pitch of the engines changes as the landing craft slows and turns toward the shore. I know that in a few seconds the big door will go down and then it is up to fate. I finger the dog tag around my neck to make sure the chain still holds. I look down at the dog tag laced into my boot. They are my best claims to identification by the burial detail.

The machine guns on top of the landing craft are silent. I can see the port side gunner lying on the deck, sighting down the barrel as he slowly swings it from side to side looking for a target. This is a good sign— no enemy target yet. Maybe they are waiting for us to enter a trap away from the protective fire of the boat's machine guns. Now I want to get away from the confines of this tin can and onto the ground where we have a chance to use our infantry tactics. Then we can deal with whatever they throw at us.

The troops unload quickly. They want to get to the ground fast. Brad and I rush off the ramp into a small patch of mud where our boots only sink a few inches. This is not too bad. The landing craft pilot did his job well. We get off without getting stuck in a long stretch of mud that sucks your boots down and makes you a sitting duck.

The land gradually rises to reveal an open field with about two hundred meters to the tree line. VC could be there waiting for us. Our soldiers spread out and run toward the tree line keeping an orderly and swiftly moving formation, well spread out. They cover the first one hundred meters in less than a half-minute. Just when it seems Mr. Charles should play his hand, a burst of automatic fire spits out from the tree line. We all hit the ground at once.

Brad and I are in the middle of the pack. Rounds whiz overhead or spit into the mud. Our troops return fire from the prone position on full automatic. It is like rock and roll with M16s, more than enough firepower to suppress the dozen or so AK-47s and old Chinese bolt action rifles that are firing at us. Our soldiers start to fire and maneuver. The base element fires in short bursts while the maneuver element runs a few meters and drops to the ground. Then they switch roles and the process repeats itself a few times. The units come up to a stream running parallel and about thirty meters away from the tree line. They momentarily come back into line. There is less enemy fire.

Our soldiers are familiar with obstacles like streams and canals. They don't wait for long. Again the base units lay down rapid suppressive fire into the enemy positions while the others rush into the stream and quickly gain the other side. There, they lay under the protection of the bank and fire the next volley of suppressive fire at the enemy. Then the rest of us follow across the stream.

I say to Brad, "Go ahead and cross. I'll cover you."

I am in the prone position with my rifle at the ready. I fire a few short bursts at muzzle flashes in the tree line. Brad slides down the stream bank, but slips under water. He comes up gasping, water cascading off his head and shoulders.

He shouts, "Lost my rifle...deep water!"

A stunning realization hangs in the space between us for a few seconds. Voices from infantry school scream in my mind. A rifleman never loses his rifle, especially...in a combat zone...in the middle of a charge against a shooting enemy. A rifleman always cares for his weapon first, before anything else. Clean your weapon, check your weapon, sleep with your weapon! If you have to run for your life, take your weapon before anything else—boots, clothes, pack, anything! If you are standing buck naked in the middle of a freezing forest, but you have your weapon, you can still fight and take on the enemy. If you have your weapon, all will be right with the world.

I imagine the same drilled-in rules are resonating in Brad's head, probably even more so, since he is a Sergeant First Class, E-7, backbone of the army, combat veteran with a Combat Infantryman Badge and all that goes with it. He is probably feeling that this is embarrassing and, worse, life threatening. How the heck are we going to get out of this one with our pride intact, let alone survive with our lives?

Snapping myself back to the situation, with Brad still wiping water from his from his head, I say, "Dive for it! Feel with your hands."

Meanwhile, I think the stream looks like it is about five feet deep, except deeper in spots, and it is over ten feet wide. I wonder how hard it is to find a rifle in the muddy water. Then Brad comes up again, gasping for breath. He is holding the rifle up with one arm and plunging for the opposite shore.

With a feeling of relief, no doubt shared by my partner, I say, "Good work, Brad!"

He lies on the mud bank taking deep breaths and checking his weapon. He fires a test shot into the enemy position.

He turns and says, "Come on over."

I take one last look at the tree line, get up, and slide feet first down the bank, land on my butt in the mud, and then into the water, all while holding my M16 over my head with one arm. My uppermost thought is to keep my rifle out of the water. That, and hoping there is no enemy surge toward our position. The water comes up to my chest and I swim over to the other side with one arm still holding the rifle. I vaguely wonder if there are any snakes or other nasty critters in the water with me.

Meanwhile our soldiers have crossed over the stream and are running on the other side. Few shots are fired from the enemy. It appears that we have them in a rout. Maybe our plan is working.

"Good going, LT." says Brad. "Let's catch up to the others"

"Roger," I say with determination and move forward only mildly aware that my sopping wet fatigues slow me down. The whole incident of the muddy creek and the lost rifle is instantly put behind us.

We are now probably forty meters behind our soldiers.

I go about ten meters...see a movement to my left out of the corner of my eye. Turning and instinctively ducking down I see an AK-47 pointing directly at me from under a covered fighting hole. Time slows down. I see the details of the situation in an instant. My rifle goes up and my mind says this is the moment you will die. It feels like an eternity as I try to swing my M16 around to fire. The AK-47 muzzle flashes and rounds hit the bottom of the tree next to me. Brad's M16 spits out a short burst of automatic fire and the figure behind the AK-47 jolts up covered in blood. He slumps forward and then falls back into his hidey-hole.

The hideout is covered with brush but I see another enemy in the hole. He does not shoot. I raise my weapon to fire but the fighter yells, "Chieu Hoi." My mind flashes the meaning, "I surrender." He holds up his weapon with one arm.

I am one fraction of an instant from blowing him to eternity, but instead shout, "Hold it Brad."

Brad drops to one knee, pointing his weapon right at the enemy, and says, "Watch out LT, it could be a trick. There could be more of them."

Dropping to one knee, I hold my aim on the VC. Brad walks up a few paces from the enemy, with rifle pointed, ready to blow Charlie away. I think the safe thing would be to get rid of this guy. After all, he and his buddy tried to blow us away. I scan the surrounding terrain and look for more hidey-holes.

I say, "Brad, we have a prisoner, a hoi chanh."

Looking at the VC, my rifle at shoulder level, pointing directly at his chest, I say, in a firm, deliberate tone, "OK, chieu hoi," and motion for him to come out of his hole.

Brad and I keep him covered while he pushes his AK-47 forward, and then crawls out of the hole. I motion for the VC to squat and he does so with hands over his head. While I cover the prisoner Brad checks around for more spider holes. The VC is dressed in black pajamas. He has a scared look in his eyes but his face reveals little emotion.

Brad returns and looks in the spider hole at the shattered fighter. His wounds bleed onto a beautiful red and blue checked scarf tied around his neck. Brad reaches down and pulls the scarf from the corpse, then walks behind the prisoner and ties his hands behind his back with it. Then he frisks the hoi chanh for weapons and papers. In addition to another thirty-round magazine of AK-47 ammo there is a map and a letter. He hands them to me as he hauls the prisoner up to his feet and motions with his rifle in the direction to move.

By this time our soldiers have cleared the area and chased Charlie away. A radio transmission from our blocking forces reports that three VC have been killed, but it appears that the rest of them have made their escape.

Back at the headquarter's fort we find three dead VC stretched out on the ground in the open area where we have also collected our few wounded soldiers. The bodies do not appear to be disfigured except for a few small punctures suggesting the cause of death. Later, soldiers bring the dead VC that tried to kill me. There are nasty, visible wounds on his face and neck from the marks of Brad's burst. Local villagers pass by and peer at the dead, perhaps looking for someone they know.

We set our prisoner down outside the fort where several soldiers guard him. We sit nearby in our usual spot on a few logs under our favorite palm tree. Trung si Sang interprets the captured map and letter for us. The map shows VC positions before our attack, and it pinpoints the positions of our two forward companies before we redeployed elements of Alpha Company for our blocking force. It also shows what may be several spider holes that we missed.

Brad says, "Maybe the holes were not used, or maybe the occupants fled, or maybe they just held tight without enough advantage to attack us."

"That may explain why our blocking force stopped only a few VC," I say.

Holding the map in one hand, and gesturing toward it with his other, Trung si Sang says, "The map is very detailed and unusual for a regular rifleman to carry."

Brad adds, "Maybe he's a leader."

"Maybe VC in other hidey-holes held back on shooting at us for fear of shooting their leader," I say.

I wonder if Brad and I were lucky to avoid further enemy fire. Maybe Brad and I would be dead men if we had not taken the prisoner.

Brad's face shows he is thinking the same thing, and he says "Whew, that might have been close...very close."

I say, "Yeah, let's ask our soldiers to go back there and check out the area again, watching out for traps, of course."

After putting the map down, Trung si Sang explains the VC letter in his hand. It is addressed to Nguyen Tat Thanh, from family located in North Vietnam. Sang reads the whole thing. I am touched by the sentiments expressed in the letter.

"Ask him if it is his," I say.

The prisoner confirms that he is Nguyen Tat Thanh, but is reluctant to talk more.

I say, "Tell him that we will send him to the rear for questioning, and if he cooperates he will get the letter back."

As Sang interprets Thanh smiles faintly and nods his head.

We talk to Dai uy Quan about the map and the letter and explain our ideas about how other VC avoided capture. He says that he wants to interrogate the prisoner and also send him to Vietnamese authorities. I reply that it may be useful for his men to question Thanh and study the map, but that we have an interest in him as our prisoner because our district and province intelligence officers are eager to question him. This is a change from what usually happens, but Dai uy Quan respects our chain of command and agrees. I am relieved at this because there are stories about how the Vietnamese have treated prisoners harshly.

Brad and I go back to sitting under our tree, drinking water from our canteens. Our fatigues are almost dry after our plunge in the stream.

"Brad," I say, "thanks for saving my life back there. I don't think I could have swung around in time to take him out."

Brad replies, "Yuh, LT, I didn't want him to ruin your day, especially after you covered me swimming for my rifle."

"Ah," I say with a smile, "you were tenacious. Good thing you found it."

He says with a bright smile, "Now LT, I may be more nine-acious or seven-acious than ten-acious."

Picking up on the silly mood, a relief from the stress of the assault, I say, "Does that mean you were not fully committed to recovering your weapon?"

"Nah, it just means that I might have dove down only seven or so times for it, and not ten."

"Ha, you get wet...you get twisted real bad." In a serious tone I say, "You saved my life. I think I owe you a drink for today."

"LT, I think you may owe me a couple of drinks for today."

"You're right, Brad, your right about that!"

Seventeen

EXPURGATION

Over the next few weeks, we push on through the Huu Dinh encountering only light resistance. We figure that our successful attack with the landing craft put the scare in Mr. Charles. Then again, it could be that Thanh and his fighting partner of late, identified as Dang Vu Hiep, were leaders, and their loss took the steam out of the resistance.

On some nights, as I swing in my hammock, I reflect back over the capture of Thanh. I think how close I came to death and how Brad saved my life. I also think how close I came to blowing Thanh away. I can still remember the pressure of my finger on the trigger, hesitating. I am glad that we gave Thanh safe passage into American hands. Recollection of his letter makes me think of his family and his humanity, even if I don't agree with his politics.

Somehow preserving Thanh gives me a good feeling, even in the face of my own brush with death. In a fraction of a second, both of our lives changed. It makes a big difference for Thanh and maybe for me too. He gets to live, and I don't bear the burden of killing him, no matter how justifiable. It feels like a small, decent act amid all this turmoil. It gives me a liberating, healing feeling. This uplifts me, washes over me in a wave of profound happiness, and cleanses my soul. It is expurgation. It helps to neutralize the offensive errors of this war and gives me hope that my own humanity has not been totally twisted.

—

As we wrap up operations in the Huu Dinh, new orders come in to relocate the team to an island south of Ben Tre, in Mo Cay District. The word is that government forces control one half of the island and Victor Charles controls the other half. This situation is very similar to our experience in the Huu Dinh. We also get word that Captain Blake's replacement will arrive after we start our assignment in Mo Cay. We say our good-byes to Thie u ta Tan, Dai uy Quan and the other men of our battalion. They know we are pleased to have served with them and that we appreciate their skills and experience as soldiers. We wish them luck on their next assignment near Saigon.

Back in the province compound, the team stands down for a few days. We sleep on genuine army bunks, chow down on good mess hall meals, and take hot showers every day. On Sunday we attend a service held by an army chaplain in the compound pavilion. The seats are full. I am not sure if it is because men are religious or because a real live chaplain is visiting. Maybe it is just a distraction or a little piece of normal existence, something to sooth the soul.

The chaplain gives a sermon about the story of mankind. Time and time again one group, tribe, state, or nation has little respect for their neighbors and does not try to understand them. Greed for the possessions and resources of others and the desire to control them leads to conflicts. The story has been repeated through the centuries with notable examples in Greek and Roman times, the Middle Ages, and on into recent history. We try to control things with the force of arms, but it just doesn't work for long. The human spirit eventually prevails, but then we forget and the demons of conflict return. The reverend wraps up by saying that it is innocent people who suffer the most, and often men who are forced to be soldiers are the ones who pay the ultimate price.

Near the close of the service, the preacher reads a prayer, "Memorial Day Prayer," written by a colleague, Reverend Barbara J. Pescan, about the sacrifices of soldiers that must be remembered. The preacher reads artfully, trying to convey feelings with inflections, pauses, and tones. At first, we soldiers squirm a bit on the benches, and then we become quiet and still, listening intently to the words:

Spirit of Life
whom we have called by many names
in thanksgiving and in anguish—
Bless the poets and those who mourn
Send peace for the soldiers who did not
make the wars
but whose lives were consumed by them

Let strong trees grow above graves far
from home
Breathe through the arms of their
branches
The earth will swallow your tears while
the dead sing
"No more, never again, remember me."

For the wounded ones, and those who
received them back,
let there be someone ready when the
memories come
when the scars pull and the buried metal
moves
and forgiveness for those of us who were
not there
for our ignorance.

And in us, veterans in a forest of a thousand fallen promises,
let new leaves of protest grow on our
stumps.

Give us courage to answer the cry of
humanity's pain
And with our bare hands, out of full
hearts,
with all our intelligence
let us create the peace.

The preacher says, "Let us pause for a moment of
silent reflection and quiet prayer."

I sit there taking it all in. The words ring true and
touch me deeply. I picture thousands of GIs marching
through this war, fighting, falling, being lost to their
families or sent home bandaged and broken. Then I see
angels of mercy gathering to hold up the wounded and
dead and many people with upturned faces looking at
a white and gold banner for peace. The images go from
dark to bright in my mind and I feel a stirring in my soul.

After a few moments the preacher says, "Blessed be."

He looks at our upturned faces and says, "For a
benediction I offer the words of Reverend Dr. Martin
Luther King Jr.: 'Peace is not merely a distant goal that
we seek, but a means by which we arrive at that goal.'
Bless you all. Go safely in these dangerous times. May
you find peace."

A postlude plays over the loudspeaker. Peter, Paul,
and Mary sing Bob Dylan's "Blowing in the Wind." I

wonder too, how many deaths it will take. I am thinking too many people have died in the mess of Vietnam
for too little good. More songs float over the air. Barry
McGuire warns of destruction if we don't act differ-
ently. The Youngbloods want us to love one another.
For a moment I feel peace is possible. I hope that all can
be cleansed of the morally harmful errors of this war!
End this war! End all war! It is a choice, just as it was a
choice to let Thanh live in spite of his murderous intent.

But I know that there are still people outside this
compound who will be happy to blow me away. I think
maybe there should be peace, maybe there is a way to
peace, but not right here and not right now. The truth
is we are in too deep. We are all out here trying to kill
each other. Larger forces have put us here. In the Nam,
we are pawns on the battlefield. I cannot let my guard
down. The old protective shield closes up inside of me.

We stand up to walk away. A chaplain's assistant
and some helpers start packing up the chaplain's kit: a
portable altar, hymnals, and religious instruments. We
help them straighten the benches in the pavilion. One
of them plays another song over the sound system. It
is the Animals, "We Gotta Get Out of This Place." The
loudspeaker blares the lyrics. They resonate with me
and probably every other GI there because we all want
out of this place.

We take a few steps away. Brad says, "Hey, that's the GI theme song."

"Yeah, the most popular song in Nam."

I snap back the lid of my Zippo, flick the spark wheel, and draw the flame into the end of a panatela. The warm smoke tastes good and creates a satisfying aroma.

Brad says, "I think the reverend's got it together! How long will the propaganda machine tolerate sermons like that? Sometimes you just wonder what makes sense."

"Yeah, Brad, it makes you wonder, especially with the things that don't add up in this war."

He says, "Yeah, and I like the prayer too...and the songs."

I reply, "Sometimes the only thing that makes sense is rock and roll. But, y'know, a prayer might be better."

"Yeah, yeah, you know what?" he says with a quirky smile. "The only thing I know for sure is...if it were any other way it would be different."

ABBREVIATED TIME LINE
VIETNAM WAR

208 BC	Start of Chinese domination over Vietnam interspersed with insurrection, revolt, or periods independence.
1428-	Periods of Vietnamese rule, civil strife, influence of French missionaries, factionalism, French military influence.
1861	French forces capture Saigon. French influence expands over Indochina.
1890	Ho Chi Minh is born in Central Vietnam.
1911	Ho leaves Vietnam for thirty years.
1918	Ho arrives in Paris as Nguyen Ai Quoc.
1919	At Versailles Peace Conference Ho unsuccessfully attempts to convince President Woodrow Wilson of self-determination for Vietnam.
1920	Ho joins French Communist party hoping for power to liberate Vietnam.
1932	Bao Dai is enthroned as emperor of Vietnam with French support.
1940	Japanese occupy Indochina during WWII.
1941	Ho Chi Minh returns to Vietnam to fight Japanese and French.

1944   Vo Nguyen Giap establishes Vietminh.

1945   Bao Dai proclaims Vietnam independence with Japanese support. Japanese surrender to Allies. Bao Dai abdicates. Ho declares the independence of Vietnam, citing French and American revolutionary declarations, but British forces (there per Potsdam Conference) return authority to French.

1946   France recognizes Vietnam as a "free state" under France.

1950   Ho Chi Minh declares that the Democratic Republic of Vietnam is the only legal government and is recognized by the Soviet Union and China. The United States and Britain recognize Bao Dai's government. President Truman sends the Military Assistance Advisory Group (MAAG) to assist the French in Vietnam.

1954   French are defeated at Dien Bien Phu. Agreements in Geneva establish the division of Vietnam at the 17th parallel pending national elections. Bao Dai denies the agreements, selects Ngo Dinh Diem as Prime Minister with US support.

1955   Diem rejects Geneva agreements, refuses to participate in nationwide elections, defeats Bao Dai in a referendum, declares the Republic of Vietnam with himself as president.

1957   Communist insurgents organize in the Mekong Delta.

1960   On January 17th, VC leader Madame Nguyen Thi Dinh leads a large scale VC uprising in Ben Tre Province, where she was born. She is a founder of the National Liberation Front, established later in the year, and called Viet Cong by the Saigon government. For many, this year is considered the start of the war with the Americans.

1962   The American Military Assistance Command is established in South Vietnam. Advisors are increased to 12,000. During his first visit to Vietnam, Secretary of Defense Robert Strange McNamara says, "...every quantitative measure...shows that we are winning the war."

1963   South Vietnamese generals carry out a coup against President Diem who is murdered the next day.

1964   In response to a 2 August attack on the American destroyer *Maddox* by North Vietnamese patrol boats; the US Congress passes the Tonkin Gulf Resolution, giving President Johnson power to act in Southeast Asia.

1965   The first American combat troops, two marine battalions, arrive on March 8 to defend Danang Airfield. Troop strength rises to 200,000.

Saving BEN TRE

1966   President de Gaulle of France calls for American withdrawal from Vietnam. He said Vietnamese independence should be "...guaranteed by nonintervention of any outside powers..." President Johnson declines to act.

1967   Surveys of American people indicate mixed sentiment toward war: many say the war was wrong in the first place but now we should either win it or get out. Fifty-five percent want a tougher policy. On February 27, after returning from Saigon, Walter Cronkite says it is "...more certain than ever that the bloody experience of Vietnam is to end in stalemate."

1968   On January 30, the North Vietnamese and VC launch the Tet Offensive by attacking cities and towns. VC invade thirteen of sixteen provincial capitals of the Mekong Delta including Ben Tre. Ben Tre is recaptured after allies decide to bomb and shell the town to smash the Viet Cong regardless of civilian casualties. The shelling is followed by fierce street fighting by the US Ninth Division. In February, McNamara leaves the post of Secretary of Defense noting the futility of the war. The My Lai Massacre occurs on March 16. American troop strength rises to 540,000.

1969   Large antiwar demonstrations take place in Washington DC. Ho Chi Minh dies in Hanoi. The Associated Press reports the My Lai massacre in November.

1970   On May 4, the Ohio National Guard kills four students at Kent State war protests. On November 12, Lieutenant William Calley goes on trial at Fort Benning, Georgia, for his role in the My Lai massacre. American troop strength declines to 280,000.

1971   On March 29, Lieutenant Calley is convicted of murdering civilians at My Lai. *The New York Times* publishes the Pentagon Papers on June 13, exposing how the public had been mislead on Vietnam by several administrations. American troop strength declines to 140,000.

1973   Henry Kissinger and Le Duc Tho reach agreement and a cease-fire is signed in Paris on January 27. American troops leave Vietnam by March 29.

1974   President Thieu announces that war has restarted.

1975   Communist forces take over key cities. They capture Saigon on April 30.

Primary Source: Stanley Karnow. *Vietnam, A History, The First Complete Account of Vietnam at War.* Viking Press, N. Y. 1983

Made in the USA
Middletown, DE
24 July 2015